Copyright 2013
Publisher: R. E. Stowell
Fairbanks, Alaska

Books by Rosalyn Stowell
Don't Use A Chainsaw In The Kitchen (cookbook)
Trilogy: PAW Novels (Post Apocalyptic World)
The Beginning - Book 1
The Dark Of Night - Book 2
The Dawn - Book 3
Alaskan Gold - Romance Novel
The Alaskan Mosquito Cookbook (humor)
Alaskan Alibi - Hunting & Suspense

Cover photo by Sam Harrel
Photo of the Writer by Samantha Stowell
Thanks to Kara Stowell for proof reading it, yet again
Interior Photos by Rosalyn Stowell
Special thanks to Arctic Athletics Association

Chapter 1

"So, are you having fun yet?" asked a man's voice from behind me, as I knelt beside my old truck, fixing the flat.

Well, I was trying to fix the flat but whoever tightened the lug nuts had used an air wrench and enjoyed his work.

I'm not a little girl, so I stood on the star wrench and rocked back and forth, then jumped from side to side and eventually, it came loose. Only 5 more to go. Damn. At least I have them loosened.

I turned around to see who thought he was a comedian and decided he probably could be whatever he wanted, he was just that good looking.

"Okay, so are you offering to help or just stand there and watch?" I sorta snarled back. It is hot and I am already tired. This has not been one of my better days and it doesn't appear to be going to get much better as it goes along.

The client I was supposed to pick up at the airport didn't show and when I called the contact number for him, a lady answered saying he was unavailable. If I got my hands on him, he certainly wouldn't be. Not getting a refund, either.

Did he think I would enjoy a little trip to town from hunt camp during my busiest season? Who wouldn't enjoy taking a 150 mile road trip on a gravel road in hot weather with all the dust and rocks? Probably a good thing he didn't show, if this was an example of his common sense and thoughtfulness for others.

Back at the flat tire, my audience decided he would lend a hand and the rest of the lug nuts just gave up and practically fell off. Yeah, not my day.

My spare is low on air, so I will have to head directly to a tire shop. Then the guy introduces himself and says my no-show sent him in his place. Okaaaay. I ask if he has the rest of the payment for the hunt and where is his gear? He says his friend was supposed to send the rest of the payment. When and how? He doesn't know.

"Uh, you do know there is no hunt with no payment, right?"

"You can just let me come on out now and the money will be here when we come back in, can't you?"

"No, it don't work that way, sorry." I start to climb back into my pickup and he grabs my shoulder. Big mistake.

He looks up at me from under my foot and asks politely for his arm back, please?

Oops, first rule in camp, don't touch me. Second rule is, don't touch me.

I let go of his arm and he slowly gets up and brushes himself off.

"How did you do that? That first lug nut must have been on there a lot harder than the rest."

"Of course, did you think I hadn't already loosened all of them before taking one completely off? Do you have a vehicle or are you hiking?"

He grabs his backpack and throws it and a duffle bag into the back of my truck and I head for the nearest tire shop.

While waiting for service, I check my laptop to see if No-Show has sent anything. Nope, nothing. I turn the screen so the Flat Changer can see his buddy has ignored sending any notice about him or cash for the rest of the hunt.

"If you are planning on going hunting, you better contact him and get it settled or you are not riding on out with me." I tell him.

He looks all hurt that I don't trust him for the money and pulls out his cell phone. Soon it sounds like he is getting the same answers I got from the guy's Secretary, Personal Assistant or whoever she is.

Finally he says something to her that gets her attention and soon he is talking to someone else, but still not the man he wanted to talk to.

While he is talking on the cell, someone changes the channel on the TV in the tire shop waiting room and we hear the name of the man he is trying to get in touch with, mentioned on the News.

Well, it seems we won't be getting the balance due on the hunt from him, he is dead. Then another picture flashes on the screen as someone they would like to talk to and my Tire Changing guy is shown, big as life and twice as handsome, right there, on the screen.

His plane ticket is sticking out of his jacket pocket, so I sorta just ease it out to see when he got here and where he came in, from.

According to this ticket stub, he came in last night and left from the Dallas/Fort Worth airport, sometime during the day, yesterday. So he isn't guilty of his friend's death. The news report is saying it happened sometime during the night and he was found in his office this morning.

I suggest this guy go directly to the State police here in Fairbanks with his ticket and get the police in Texas looking for someone else besides him. He agrees and then gives me a hard look for having his ticket in my hand.

He didn't have to leave the tire shop, having given his name to the person in Texas, they evidently called our police and they were already here to talk to him. Whoever the man in Texas had been, he must have been important to someone.

I still have his ticket when the police grab onto him and cuff him. They read him his Rights immediately. I recognize one of the police officers and ask to speak to him.

We step outside and I ask why they cuffed and read him his Rights, thought they only wanted to talk to him from the report on the news.

Officer Reed tells me he can't talk about the case. I ask if he knows when this guy got here, when he left Texas and when the victim was killed. He says he has only the last part of that information, so I hand over the ticket I have. He looks at me and asks how I got it, so I tell him. He hands it back after looking at it. He did write down the information on it to check and make sure that really is when this guy got here. I would imagine there is a hotel listing him as an overnight guest somewhere here in town, also.

When we walk back in, Officer Reed tells the others to let him go. He has a pretty good alibi for the time involved. One of the men snickers and makes a rather crude remark about me and the guy's alibi, I take a step toward him. His eyes widen and Officer Reed tells him he WILL apologize and immediately or he will let me teach him some manners. He apologizes.

Tire Dude tells him to just pat me on the shoulder and snickers. Officer Reed gives him a hard look, too.

Okay, Tire Dude has a name. He is Cary Lowny. His deceased friend is none other than William Garrison The Third. Everyone always spoke of him in capitols. Didn't help, he is still dead. When he made the reservation for our hunt, he just said Will Garrison, so I didn't even think The William Garrison The Third would be booking a hunt with me.

I don't advertise full service hunting trips, I just advertise primitive hunt camps and the chance to see a bear. No promises on getting one. Usually folks like The Third want better facilities and practically someone to pull the trigger for them, which I don't do, either. Okay, that isn't fair. I never met the man and have preconceived notions. Not nice, even, he can't defend himself.

After the police leave, Cary pulls out his wallet and asks how much is still owed for the hunt. He doesn't even blink and just starts signing over travelers checks. The shop guy comes in and says my pickup is ready to go, so we head on out to it.

I pull in at my bank and deposit the travelers checks. They won't do me much good out in the Bush.

I pull out the standard guide client form and waiver for Cary to sign and also take him in to buy his license and tags. He signs the hunt contract I have to turn in to the State, also.

He is laughing as he reads the waiver I have included at the bottom of the client form. I tell him it isn't so funny when some snooty client wants to sue me for getting his butt bit by bugs while using the outhouse. So I try to cover all bases in the waiver.

Chapter 2

We are almost out of cell range when his phone goes off again. I pull over so he doesn't lose service and he is trying to calm someone down on the other end of the phone. Seems it is the grieving widow. Seems she is on her way here and is about to land at the Fairbanks airport. Also seems she wants to go with us. What the heck?

He asks me nicely and crosses my palm with several Ben Franklins and we turn around and head back to the airport.

My first impression of her is a bit jaundiced. Think starlet appearing in front of cameras at a premier and you would have Sheila Garrison down to a T. The big sunglasses didn't do much to camouflage her, either. Since she left them on in the terminal, she almost fell down the stairs from the unloading zone to the ground floor. The drinks she had managed along the trip up didn't help any, either. Her first words were, "Where's a bar? I need a drink."

I'm supposed to allow this piece of fluff to come

with us out to bear camp? Well, it might entertain the bears.

I look at Cary and quietly ask, "You are kidding, right?"

He says no, he will take care of her. You bet he will. I don't babysit and no booze will be brought into camp. Guns and alcohol don't mix. I tell him this and he frowns but agrees. She might have a hard few days, since it seems she lives on the stuff.

So now we are going to be a combo hunt camp and drunk rehab center. I don't think he paid me enough for this. I am glad I don't have any other clients scheduled for this week.

I make her sign a client waiver release form, also, although in her current condition, I don't know how binding it would be.

If what she is wearing is the type of clothing she has packed in all those bags, she is going to truly hate us and everything about hunt camp. High heeled strappy sandals, short flirty skirts and dresses, halter tops and little jackets.

I stop at wally world and send him in to pick up some cheap boots and sweats, at least. She will hate it, but she won't be as uncomfortable. I don't want to leave her unattended in my truck.

She is passed out in the back seat, so after he comes out, I go pick up some perishable goods for our meals and we are soon on the road toward camp.

I wonder why she is here, instead of home taking care of whatever must need taking care of now.

Cary says no, the Administrative Assistant has everything under control and that Sheila has no say in how anything gets done, even though she is the widow. Somehow, that is sad.

Next, I wonder if the police know where she is. Well, not really my worry. I point out a cow and calf moose as we drive along and Cary is fascinated by them. They are the first ones he has ever seen.

I hear Sheila waking up in the back seat and pull over to the side of the road and have the back door open before she gets upright and decides she needs to barf in my truck. Cary gets the other side door open and we watch to see which way to pull her as she sways upright. Cary is the lucky one and grabs her out before she can make a mess on the truck or him. When he calls her Sis, I wonder if she is an actual sister or if that is just a pet name. Not that I am interested.

I pull in to a gravel pit for Cary to do some shooting before we reach the hunting area. I need to see how good a shot he is and what he has brought to shoot with. He opens his duffle bag and pulls out a locked handgun case. He opens another bag and pulls out the box of ammo for the handgun. It is a single shot Thompson Contender. He has a .308 barrel on it.

He is a pretty good shot and is familiar with his weapon, so it should be okay. Sheila is covering her ears and complaining of a headache. Too bad.

By the time we reach camp, she is a mess, shivering and shaking. Just how much does she usually drink and are we going to kill her by making her quit cold turkey?

Cary thinks it will be good for her, I think I need my head examined for allowing her to come out here, probably him too.

She crawls into a tent as soon as we reach camp and is soon out, again. I stuff a large heavy duty bag into her hand as she goes in, telling her to use that to barf in, or she will be buying all new gear for me. She mumbles okay.

Cary thinks maybe I am a little rough on her, I tell him I grew up around drunks, I don't have to put up with them now.

I prepare dinner and he wakes her up to eat. She is whiney and only wants a drink. I hand him a bottle and she starts chugging it down before it dawns on her it is plain water. She gives me an evil look and plops down in one of the camp chairs. Oh, this is going to be such a fun week.

He does not want to leave her in camp by herself this first night so declines going out hunting. It is light all night, so she is complaining about the light. I throw a quilt over her tent to darken it some and tell her goodnight.

I am tired and not sure what I have let myself in for on this hunt. I go ahead and go to my tent. He can babysit her tonight if he wants. Not part of my job description.

Once in a while through the night, I hear her barfing and him murmuring to her. He really is patient with her.

By the next evening, I am ready to use her for bait at one of the bait stations. She is a steady stream of complaints. She doesn't like breakfast, she doesn't like her tent, she doesn't like her sleeping bag and she doesn't like the sweats and boots but she really don't like the outhouse or the bugs.

She has the shakes and is having trouble walking on the uneven ground. She wants to know where the shower is and where she can buy a bottle. That one is easy, about 150 miles back that direction, pointing vaguely southeast.

She finally just sits down on the ground and starts crying. I hand Cary a package of wet wipes and he mops up her face and she starts flinching away from his wash job. As he wipes off the makeup, bruises in various stages of healing show up on her face. When he pushes up her sleeve and washes her arm, there are bruises all over her wrists, also. She looks like someone systematically beat on her and quite often, at that.

Before she notices, I click a few pictures to show what her face looks like. Without the makeup, she looks very young.

I ask her how and why she decided to fly up here at this time and she says the Administrative Assistant, John McCready, suggested it that morning right after Will's body was found. He said he would handle everything for her. He even had her bags packed and ready for her to catch her flight north.

Something doesn't seem right here. I suggest she not open those bags at all until we go back to town and let the police open them. Cary agrees. She says she might as well, she don't +own anything suitable for out here, anyway.

We lock her bags in my pickup. I will keep the keys on me. As we get ready to go check one of the bait stations, someone hallo's the camp.   It is Officer Reed and his partner. This is definitely not a common occurrence in my hunt camp, so I immediately think it has something to do with Sheila or Cary.

Officer Reed is looking at all the bruises on Sheila and quietly points them out to his partner. She nods and asks Sheila if she is okay and does she have more bruises on the rest of her body like the visible ones? She drops her head and says yes, very quietly. We get Sheila to tell the Troopers what she told us about why she was here and how she came to be here. They were nodding their heads as she progressed. We told them we had her unopened bags locked in my pickup. They perked up their ears at that.

They asked her permission to open the bags, so we all trouped out to my pickup and I unlocked the doors.. They took pictures the entire time we removed the bags, placed them on the tailgate and they opened each one, and catalogued the contents.

The main item of interest was a blood soaked knife wrapped in one of her silk shirts. It had paper around it also, and no one touched any of it, using gloves and placing each item in an evidence bag, tagging it and logging it into their book.   They take all our fingerprints also, just to compare with any they might find.

If Sheila had opened the bag and pawed through it, she would have left fingerprints all over everything. Maybe something was finally going her way.

I think the officers believe her as they don't haul her away and that is usually a good sign. They do take her luggage all in with them.

She is still shaking from no booze, but not quite as bad. This has shocked her into thinking of something else.

We might as well spend the evening at a bait station, looking at bears. It might keep her mind off her problems.

We take the pickup a few miles away from camp and park it. Then we hike farther into the woods. As much noise as both of them are making, we will be lucky to see anything tonight, but he is paying, so we will go sit and watch.

I look at the bait set up and see that it has been used since I last checked before I went to town to pick up The Third.

I get them settled in fairly comfortably and motion to be quiet. They finally comply and we sit quietly for almost an hour before there is movement out through the trees. I quietly get their attention and point. They watch as a sow and small twin cubs come in to the bait. The sow would not be coming in openly like this if there were any males in the area, so tonight will be only bear viewing. Sheila has her camera out and snapping pictures almost fast enough for video. She is so excited she isn't even shaking. Her hands aren't too steady, so I am not sure how good the photos will be, but she is enjoying the evening and so is Cary.

The cubs are playing and running around while their mother eats from the bait station. Then her head comes up and she is sniffing the air and getting nervous. I caution Cary and Sheila to be quiet and pay attention now, there may be a male coming in. The sow looks back the way they came in and woofs to her cubs. They immediately come to her and then they all take off in the other direction instead of the way they came in.

I have my gun at the ready and motion for Cary to do the same. Soon, we see the back of a very large bear, walking toward the bait station, following the trail of the sow and cubs. If a male finds them, he tries to kill the cubs as then the sow will come back into heat, for mating. Otherwise, it is a couple of years between mating.

This looks like a very large boar. He dwarfs the bait barrel. He sniffs around the barrel and finally takes a pawful to munch on. He is much more interested in the scent left behind by the sow. I motion to Cary that this is indeed a trophy sized male if he is interested in taking it.

As Cary lifts his handgun, the bear evidently spots the movement. Even though they may not have the sharpest eyesight, they can spot any movement. He turns toward us and raises the hackles on his neck and shoulders, making him look much larger than he already is. Sheila is ready to crawl under her seat.

I have warned her that she must hold still, but I am not sure she is going to manage it. Cary is waiting for a perfect shot since he only has a single shot. He might be rethinking that, about now, but a little bit late on that.

The bear decides we are not all that interesting and finally turns broadside giving Cary his chance. He places his shot perfectly and the bear drops like a stone. So does Sheila. We were not actually planning on getting a bear tonight. But sometimes that doesn't work out as planned. We wait a little while to make sure and then walk over to check out the bear. I walk up from behind and use a long stick to reach over and poke it's eye. I certainly don't want it to only be unconscious and come to while we are skinning it. That would really ruin the whole evening for all of us.

We drag the bear back to the pickup. He is far too big to carry. Then I go back to the bait station and clean it all up.

We gut the bear after starting the main cuts to make a nice shaped rug from the hide. It is late enough in the season that we don't have to salvage the meat and it smells a bit. I wouldn't want to have to eat it. Neither would either client.

While we are skinning it, a couple stop by and ask about the meat, so we give it to them. We take the partly skinned hide back to camp, I salt it heavily and will finish skinning the head and feet tomorrow.

I am tired. So are Sheila and Cary. We all head to bed after washing up from handling the bear.

By the next day, Sheila is doing much better and not shaking as much. Now they have the option of staying out here the rest of the week or going back to town, since he has gotten his bear. They opt to stay.

I finish skinning out the head and feet and rough clean the skull to hold for checking it in at Fish & Game to be measured and tagged. I flesh the hide even better, although it is fairly nicely skinned. I ask Cary what he plans on doing with the hide. He looks blank so I hand him my taxidermy brochure.

The next day, we decide to go turn in the hide and skull and get them tagged, then to the local tannery in Fairbanks. They would both like to soak at the hot springs near town, so we plan on spending the night out there. I pack the tents and sleeping bags just in case they are booked solid as they usually are.

We take care of the town stuff fairly quickly and purchase some food to take with us. The hot springs rooms are all booked, but we enjoy the springs anyway and Cary buys us dinner in their dining room. They grow most of their vegetables in greenhouses heated by the hot springs.

Then we go find a place to camp for the night. It doesn't take long to set up camp and we are soon out for the night.

We go back up to the hot springs for most of the next day, too. The hot water seems to have soaked the rest of the alcohol out of Sheila and she isn't

shaking and feels fairly good. Her bruises have
faded even more and there were some very bad ones
on her body that showed in her swimsuit and looked
like even more were under it.

They only have one more full day so I suggest the
museum at the University. We do go back to the hot
springs for a soak and swim in the morning, before
heading back to town.

They seem to enjoy the museum and then I take
them around town to find a hotel for the night.
Their flights leave the next day, but not together.
We go check at the airport and they manage to
rearrange the schedule a bit and now they are leaving
together. It looked like quite a bit of cash changed
hands during that little talk at the counter.

For just having lost her husband and his best
friend, they don't seem to actually miss The Third.
He is never mentioned and they never act like they
mourn his passing. If he was responsible for all her
bruises, I can see why she might not miss him very
much. But if it was my best friend and he had given
me this hunt in his place, as his friend, I would at
least try to seem a bit sad that he is gone.

I drop them off at the hotel they were booked at,
and leave. They were nice enough and I felt sorry
for her getting beat on, but I just couldn't relax and
enjoy their company. That's not surprising, as I
don't relax around many people and certainly don't
enjoy being around most of them.

Chapter 3

Later in the evening, I pick up my next clients and we head on out to the camp, after all the paperwork is done and signed. I already have the weeks shopping done, so we only have to stop so they can purchase their licenses and tags.

After our stop at the gravel pit to sight in their guns and so I can gauge their skills with their weapons, we park, hike in to camp and I start a fire in the fire ring. While they relax, I prepare some dinner.

We spend a peaceful evening, they have their hunting stories to tell and I am a willing listener. Usually, I can learn a lot about what kind of client they will be by what type of story they tell.

Everyone sleeps in the next morning and we spend a lazy day in camp. We have an early dinner and then head out for another bait station, farther out than the one I took Cary and Sheila to.

We park out along the road and hike in quite a ways to the station. The sign around the station show plenty of use.

Shortly after we get comfortable, there is

movement off to the right and we start paying better attention. This is not good, it is a very large grizzly. It is illegal to shoot a grizzly over bait and usually once a grizzly starts using a bait station, no black bears will come to it. We have to be very still and quiet, and hope the bear does not decide to take offense that we are here.

One of the men has a video camera and he has it on the entire time the grizzly is pacing around the bait and eating. The bear looks us over from a distance but does not come over to get a first hand look, for which I am thankful.

We wait a while after the bear is out of sight and then head back to the pickup. The bear has left his mark on the pickup, showing disapproval of our being in his territory. The right side of the truck is scratched deeply down the whole door.

Oh, I can see the home insurance company agent looking over this report now. The local one won't hardly bat an eye, but somewhere in some large city, someone will think we are pulling a fast one.

W go back to camp and I scratch that bait station for the rest of the season. The client with the camera is so excited he is playing and replaying the video. I mention he might want to keep some battery life as there isn't any way to charge them, out here.

The next evening, we get one very nice large male and take care of it. Two nights later, the other fellow gets his bear and he is happy that he saved some battery life. He got good video of his friend getting his bear and his friend took video of him getting his. The grizzly was still the highlight of their trip.

I finish skinning, fleshing and salting the hides and skulls. We have an earlier evening of it and are all in our tents before 10 pm.

When we get up and around the next morning, Cary is sitting in a chair by the fire pit and Sheila is asleep in the empty tent. What the heck?

I could get tired of these people very quickly. Cary smiles at me like I am his long lost buddy and I growl at him. As my clients come out of their tents, dragging their gear, we set about loading the pickup. I take all my gear in my backpack also.

I am not leaving anything personal here if these two are here. We planned on breakfast at the truck stop on the way in, so are ready to leave in short order. Cary looks surprised, like I am supposed to be catering to him or something. I am polite but firm. These are my current clients and they take precedence, I will be coming back with new clients, they also will come first. I tell him that as we are pulling out to leave and he is still looking baffled.

Too bad, I only have a few weeks to make a year's living and I can't drop paying clients to babysit. Both of these fellows want me to handle their trophies, so that will help on the year's income, also.

We turn the hides and skulls in to be measured and tagged, then over to the tannery and drop them off. We finish all the paperwork and I take them to their hotel.

Then I stop over at my car insurance agent's office and show him my pickup. He takes a picture and writes down the information. He is smiling as he goes back in.

I am really tired. I would love to just rent a room and sleep until next week. The new clients coming in will be my last spring hunt clients. I am so ready for this to be over for a while. Working by myself, I still have to follow the same rules and regulations as the large companies. The same insurance, the same leasing of property that we can't keep others off from, although we have to pay to walk over it. It gives me a headache, just thinking about it.

I splurge and rent a room in a much cheaper hotel and go straight to bed and sleep. Too early, there is a loud knocking that can only be described as a cop knock, on my door. What the heck?

I grab my pants and shirt and am hopping into the pants as I head for the door. The shirt is a pull over, so that works and I am decently covered as I pull open the door.

Officers Reed and Porter are standing there. I invite them in and go plop onto the bed. Officer Porter asks if I know where Cary Lowny and Sheila Garrison are?

I tell them I left them sitting in my camp, they had shown up sometime during the night and helped themselves to a tent and I left as soon as my clients and I got up, so never actually talked to them except to tell them I was coming back with clients and they needed the tents. I have no idea how they got there or why they came back. There was no vehicle parked near my pickup.

I ask why they are interested enough to come wake me up and they tell me they can't discuss ongoing investigations. Besides, it is 8 am and I need to be getting around to meet my new clients soon. Gee, thanks for the wake up call.

What should I do if Cary and Sheila are still at my camp? Are they actually wanted? Officer Reed says they will be driving out that way when they leave here, not to worry about it.

I really hate being told not to worry about something. I then always start worrying about whatever it is.

I manage to get to the airport on time to pick up the new clients. We do the paperwork thing and I get the balance of my fee. Then it is stop and get their licenses and tags and we are on our way. To celebrate my last spring clients, I stop at the truck stop for a late breakfast, since I haven't had one yet today.

I think maybe I am going to be really glad these are my last clients for a while. It is a father/son duo and they seem to have issues. Sonny boy is an overage spoiled little boy and Poppa Dearest is already drunk as a skunk and not sure how he managed that on an airplane.

When we get to camp, I manage to drop his luggage as hard as I can on the rocks I have parked beside and there is a satisfying sound of breaking glass inside. The fumes wafting up are almost enough to make me drunk just inhaling them.

Poppa is furious and Sonny boy is smirking. I'm thinking this is going to be a very long week. Poppa starts to say something and I tell him straight out, no booze in camp. I told them that on the phone and it is stated in my brochures. Guns and booze don't mix. Not in my camp, anyway.

I let Poppa carry his soggy luggage and Sonny has his in hand as we hike in to camp. I have my backpack and a bag full of groceries. Camp is deserted, so I point out the tents they can choose from and put my pack in mine. The cook tent is set up a ways from the sleeping tents and I take the bag of groceries over to it. I have metal boxes and barrels with clamp on lids to keep the groceries in. So far, I have not had a problem with bears coming into camp looking for food.

We will not be hunting this evening, as Poppa is still too under the influence to be trusted with a gun, in my opinion. I didn't even stop at the gravel pit to check out their guns and their shooting ability. We will drive back there in the morning to check that out.

Poppa manages to jostle against my tent on his way to his, when we are all getting ready for bed. I ignore him and he keeps going and muttering under his breath. I awaken several hours later to the tent being bumped again, rather roughly and push against the wall of it as it caves in toward me.

I am out of my sleeping bag and punch the tent wall just as hard as I can and hear a startled Oof. I punch it again 2 or 3 times for good measure, then grab my handgun and out the tent door in time to see a medium sized black bear running away from the camp. My startled clients are peering out their tents and after that, they are much more respectful around me. Sonny boy says he didn't think anyone punched out a bear and lived to tell the tale. He said my last punch rolled the bear over and it turned and ran. Well, heck, I thought it was one of them being funny.

The rest of the week went better than I expected after the rocky start. They both were pretty good shots and we went out checking bait stations that evening.

We saw a few smaller bears but nothing large enough to shoot on the first night hunting. One good thing about a bait station, you get to really check over any bear before shooting, so only get the large old males, usually. The clients enjoyed watching the bears and got some very good photos. One nice thing about daylight 24/7 is being able to take photos all night with no problem. Makes it simpler for hunting, also.

The third night out, a very large male came in on the bait and the son told his dad to shoot it. The dad wanted the son to shoot it, I told them to make up their minds as the bear wasn't going to wait around forever. They both turned as the bear started away from the station and fired at the same time, so they both got the bear. The Dad tagged it.

While skinning it out, I showed them exactly

where their shots had hit and both were good shots. So it wasn't clear who actually got the bear. They were both happy with it though. We took lots of photos before skinning with both of them and the bear.

They wanted to try bear meat so we salvaged part of it, even though it didn't smell all that good. It is really too late in the season for good meat.

When we get to camp, I start it soaking in water with baking soda in it, to help on the flavor. In the morning, I put it in marinade after rinsing it. Later in the day, I put some potatoes baking in the coals of the campfire and make a salad. Then I cut some sticks and peel them for them to toast their bear meat over the fire on. I will stick with salad and a potato.

The men both enjoy their bear meat dinner and I enjoy my potato. When we head for a bait station this evening, we hope to find another nice large old male.

The first bears in are a large female with a cub. She is very large and plush fur. Sonny boy wants to shoot her. I ask if he sees the cub and he says yeah. I explain in great detail what would happen if he shot a sow with cub. Besides my kicking his butt, he would have to turn the hide in to Fish & Game and would lose it besides getting a heavy fine. I would have to tell them he shot it against my advice and after being told the consequences. I am not losing my license over him wanting an illegal bear.

Poppa is taking pictures of the sow and her cub

and enjoying watching them. Our discussion has been intense but very quiet. The sow stops and looks at us once in a while, but she decides we are not a threat and continues eating.

Sonny boy starts to bring his rifle back up and I gently press a pressure point on his neck. He lowers his rifle. I tell his dad we are done hunting for the night. It is still fairly early and he wants to know why so I tell him if Sonny boy can't behave, he needs to go home. I unload Sonny's rifle and hand it back to him. Poppa doesn't have a gun with him tonight, he has already tagged his bear. So I have the only loaded weapon as we start back to the pickup. Sonny boy is furious.

I can expect to have a complaint filed against me over this one. I think I will check with other guides he may have hunted with in the past and see if he is known for this.

When we reach camp, I am surprised to see Officers Reed and Porter waiting for us. Sonny boy starts in complaining to them immediately about how I treated him. Teri raises her eyebrow at me and eases over beside me. I tell her exactly what happened and she is smiling as she walks back over to the men. She asks Poppa if he was taking photos and he is so proud of his photography he says yes and turns it on to show her what he has taken.

He is pointing out the sow and cub he took this evening. She comments on the fine pelt on the sow and Sonny boy pipes up with it was the best he had ever seen and he wanted it. She shakes her finger at him and says no, very illegal and they would have been hauling him in for a game violation if he had shot her.

He whines just like a little kid when he says he really wanted that pelt. She sweetly tells him pouting isn't attractive on a grown man.

I don't think I will get a recommendation from these two or a tip. I certainly don't want to give Sonny boy back his ammunition and let him have a gun behind me while we are walking through the woods. While the Troopers are still here, I tell my clients they are going back to town, to get packed. The son gets huffy, he hasn't got his bear yet.

Now that the dad is sober, he is fairly reasonable to deal with so I explain why the hunt is over. He looks at his son and agrees that they should go back to town. While they are packing, Officer Reed asks if I have seen anything of Cary and Sheila. I have not, so they ask if I would like them to stick around until we are ready to go out to the pickup and I say yes, I would like that very much. He has written down everything the son and the dad had said about the hunt and why it was ending now. I'm just glad they showed up when they did tonight. I had a bad feeling about the rest of the evening if I was here by myself with Sonny boy and his Poppa.

We all walked out to my pickup and their patrol vehicle. I pull out ahead of them and Sonny boy sulks in the back seat. The drive to town is very quiet. I ask Poppa which hotel he prefers and if he will want to go over to have the hide sealed in the morning to take with him.

He is thinking it over when we pull in to the hotel and Officers Reed and Porter pull in behind us. They tell us they will see us right here in the morning as they had some other questions for everyone. Now what, and it does give Sonny boy and Poppa something to think about overnight. I drop them off and go back to the cheap place I stay at.

Morning gets here way to soon after the short night I just had. But no use putting off whatever is going to be next. At least I didn't have any more clients for this season. I pick up Poppa and we head on over to Fish & Game to get the hide and skull sealed.

Officers Reed and Porter meet us there. They are disappointed that Sonny boy didn't come with us. They wanted to see how he explained his wanting to shoot a sow with a cub to these people. So did I, but Poppa left Sonny sleeping in his room he said, and since he was the only one with a bear, he is the one that came along to take care of it. Yes, but I think the Troopers were speaking to both of them last night.

While we are talking to the folk at the desk and the troopers, a call comes in and the desk person says "Oh, they are right here, sir, do you wish to speak to them?"

She hands the phone to Officer Reed and he tells the person to come right over.

Sonny boy hops out of a taxi out front a few

minutes later and is surprised to see us all standing there waiting for him when he comes through the door.

He starts right in on how incompetent I am as a Guide and he thinks they should pull my license and refund his money since he didn't get his bear.

He goes on about what a magnificent animal it had been, the best pelt he ever saw, a true trophy. All I say is, "With a cub."

Everyone turns back to him, like they are watching a tennis match.

He is practically screaming by now, "It was MY bear."

I just say, "With a cub." And he is off and ranting.

Wow, bet he was a fun date.

Chapter 4

After Sonny boy finished his tantrum in the main office, we were ready to leave. I think most are wondering why he isn't part of the food chain by now. I'm hoping they add notes to his complaint against me.

Sonny expects me to give him a ride back to the hotel, is he for real? I give his dad a ride, I leave Sonny standing in the parking lot. His dad gives me an odd look but doesn't say anything. I am glad to drop him and his trophies at the hotel. I do not offer him a taxidermy brochure. He can get everything done on his own. Hope he has fun getting the skull on as luggage, it is not cleaned well.

I head back to my camp to finish cleaning it all up and moving back home. I am tired and would love to sleep a week or two.

Since I keep a clean camp, it is easy to clean up and pack everything into my pickup. By the time I am done, the only sign I have had a camp here for several weeks is the flat areas where the tents were set up. It won't take long for them to blend in, either. I take a few photos just for my own reference and head for home.

After I unpack and make sure all the tents are well dried, I pack them away in my small shed. I head for the house and everything looks okay. For some reason, I lock the door behind me as I go in. Odd, I never lock my doors when I am home. I must just be jumpy from the last few days. Maybe I need to find someone that would like to work as an assistant guide just to have backup when I am out in the field with clients. Usually I have no problems, this spring hasn't been a normal one.

I slowly wake up to someone trying to open my door. Then I am awake instantly. I'm disoriented and find I have been sleeping at the table. My neck has a kink in it and someone is still trying to jimmy my door open.

I walk over in sock feet and pull open the door with my pistol in my hand, aimed right in the middle of whoever is trying to break in. Cary almost knocks Sheila and some other guy off the porch trying to get some distance between me and his belly.

"Okay, I've had enough of both of you. Your hunt is over, go home. Did you ever hear of knocking on a door to get someone to answer it? Picking my lock is not the way to show friendship."

I don't lower my gun, even knowing who it is. I have no reason to trust them and how did they even find my home?

I sit down on the top step and still loosely holding

the gun in their general direction, I want some answers. "Okay, first, why are you back in Alaska?"

Neither one says anything. Finally the other guy speaks up. "Hi. I'm John McCready, Administrative Assistant to William Garrison The Third, recently deceased."

"So? Is that supposed to perk up my ears and make me happy to see you? I don't care if you are Mother McCready and living in a shoe, why are all of you here and why are you trying to break into my home?"

He must be used to folks knowing who the heck that was and having it mean something to them. The guy was dead and these three were supposed to be in Texas, handling his estate and mourning the death of husband/brother-in-law/employer. Maybe even just planning how to spend all of his money. Not here in my yard, trying to break into my house.

No one jumps right in to answer. You would think they would have cooked up some story no matter if it was a lie, to tell once they got here. I back into the house and lock the door again, behind me. I don't trust any of them. I dig out my riot gun and load it up. It is scarier than the small handgun.

The next time they come to the door, they tap gently on it. I answer with the riot gun held along my side, ready to use. I back over to the table and they sit down on the couch. If I had hackles, the hair would be raised on them and I would be growling.

"Okay, I'm waiting. What kind of story have you

finally decided to tell me?"

The Assistant must figure I was not impressed so he keeps quiet. Sheila is trying to work up some tears. Cary is trying to get his charming smile to work. Finally he blurts out that they need a place to stay and want to rent a cabin from me. I ask "Why, are the police after you?"

I think Sheila is going to pass out. She has certainly forgot about squeezing out any tears. I must have hit close to home on that one. I tell them I don't have any rentals at present, sorry.

They silently troop out the door and I go lock it again, after them. Just to be on the safe side I put the little alarm under the edge of the door. It is loud enough to wake me up in the back of the house.

I check out the window and write down the license plate number and make of vehicle they are driving. With any luck, as often as I have seen the police in the last few weeks, I can hand over this information in case they really are looking for these folks. Soon, I hope.

So many questions are buzzing around in my brain I don't think I will ever get to sleep this night. So I am surprised to wake up to a lovely sunshiny day.

I forget the alarm under the door and scare myself silly when I pull the door open and it goes off. Yes, I believe it would wake me up no matter where I am sleeping.

I keep the riot gun strapped over my shoulder and a handgun on while working in the yard and tilling the garden. I have so much work to get caught up on. It's not all that comfortable, but I feel better having it on me. Once I get the rows cleared between them, in the garden, I start pulling weeds in the rows themselves. By the time I quit, the garden looks much better and I feel like I will never stand up straight again.

Dinner is leftovers from camp and I am ready for bed. I hear a vehicle pull in and check out the window. Since it is Officers Reed and Porter, I leave the riot gun by my chair when I go answer the door.

"Okay, you guys are showing up everywhere. I like your company and all, but what is the matter? I've seen you more often in the last few weeks than I have in the last several years."

They ask if I have seen Cary and Sheila and I say, "Yes, as a matter of fact, I have and they have a weasel with them named McCready. Insulting a cute little animal there by calling him a weasel."

I hand them the paper with the license number and vehicle make on it. Then told them these idiots were trying to pick my lock while I was in the house, then asked to rent a cabin from me.

Officer Reed asked if I had a cabin to rent and I said yes, I actually did. He wanted to know if I would be willing to rent it to them if they come back by and after he and Officer Porter place some surveillance in it first?

I tell him I really don't want to as they actually scare me.

They talk to me a while and ask if they both

stayed, only under cover, if I would rent out the cabin?

I mention the little detail that Cary and Sheila have both seen them. They think if they are dressed in every day work clothes and helping around the place no one will even recognize them. Teri will dye her hair a bit or just leave it down. She pulls off her hat and shakes out her hair. She does look different. He says he will shave his head and let his beard grow. Well, maybe.

She giggles and says at least I would get some help on catching up on work around here now that the spring hunts are over. Okay, that works.

She pushes her hair back under her hat and they leave. They will go get work clothes, and his old truck.

When they pull in a few hours later, I almost don't recognize them and I know them quite well. They park over near the small cabins I sometimes rent out. We spend an hour or so cleaning cabins and they set up their equipment in one of the cabins and the bugs in one of the other cabins. The third cabin is in need of too much work. Jim will stay in the cabin with the equipment, Teri will stay in the house with me and the other cabin will be available if they show up again.

We start in on my firewood supply for winter. Jim and Teri each brought their own chainsaws so we can cut wood by the truck load fairly fast. Sure enough, by the second day while we are hauling a load up to the yard, here comes Cary, Sheila and

John. They proceed more slowly when they see that I have others helping. Jim backs the pickup up to the stack and we all start pitching out firewood. We are all tired and dirty, so we look well used. No one gives Jim or Teri a second look and they just keep tossing out firewood. I walk over to see what they want this time and do not act too friendly. They will not expect me to suddenly be sweetness and light and would get suspicious if I did.

Cary asks if I would reconsider renting to them. I tell him I have managed to get one of the cabins in decent enough shape it can be rented, yes. I name the price by the night or by the week. There is nothing included in the cabin rental. No meals, no bedding, no firewood and no cutting wood on my property. I ask if they want to look in the cabin first, to see just what they are asking for.

The pickup is unloaded by now, so we drive over and they follow along behind. Jim and Teri go into Jim's cabin and we go into the cleaned up cabin. There is 2 rows of bunks along two of the walls with a partial partition between for some privacy. A curtain is hung in front of the bunks to pull across for more privacy. There is a small propane cook stove and a very small wood heater. There is an outhouse out back to be shared with the other cabin users.

I think this is more primitive than they expected. Sheila looks in shock, McCready looks appalled. Cary seems to have expected this. After all, it is better than camping in a tent was. He says they will take it. I pull out the paperwork and the key. More waivers for all of them to sign and a deposit to pay.

Teri and I walk back over to the house. We are ready to quit for the day on wood cutting and hauling. We have an impressive stack to show for it, too.

We take turns using my little outdoor shower. She is not impressed but it is better than nothing. Jim has food supplies in his cabin, so will fend for himself. Teri and I prepare a simple meal and decide what we should do tomorrow.

Hopefully, Jim will hear all he needs to hear, tonight and we won't have to do this for long.

He didn't. They went to sleep right after they had a meal, also. Jim was the only one up most of the night and he dozed off and on most of it, too.

Chapter 5

Each of the cabins faces a different direction, so no one could really see anyone entering or leaving, or even see in through the main window. So it is easy for Teri to give Jim a break now and then. The cabin they are in does have a very small vent hole in the back wall that they can use to watch the other cabin from, if they don't mind perching on a top bunk on their knees.

Sheila seems to have stayed off the booze, so that is good. McCready follows her around like a lap puppy. I'm not sure what to make of her. She certainly isn't a grieving widow. Cary still calls her Sis.

They seem to leave for a while every evening, then are back in about 4 hours. I think they are going to the truck stop for food and showers. Or not.

After a week of this, we are ready to just kick them out. They want something daily and I had told them they supply their own sleeping bags, food and firewood. Jim and Teri want to get back to their usual job.

The renters are an irritating presence in my usually fairly tranquil life. The most I usually have to deal with is an occasional bear or moose wandering through my yard. I would rather have the bears and moose than these folks. Bears are intelligent and scary, these folks are sneaky, possibly intelligent and scary. I wish they had picked somewhere else to hang out. Preferably in Texas.

They must have decided I wasn't the best host in the world and they have gone. Jim and Teri are back on their usual jobs and they didn't get any conclusive evidence in their time out here. Lots of small hints around and about the subject but not enough to do any real good. They will share what they do have with the officials in Texas just in case that is where these folks show up next.

Well, they won't have to worry about where John McCready will show up. He showed up face down in the Chena River near the riverboat landing. Sure gave that day's tour a jolt.

Now there is a lot of interest in the whereabouts of Cary and Sheila. They seem to have just disappeared. No record of them flying out from the International Airport in Fairbanks. I have a hard time picturing Sheila roughing it for very long, out anywhere in the woods.

Chapter 6

I am adding on to my woodshed. It holds over a year's worth of firewood, but I would like to have even more on hand.

I am putting in another corner post for the structure and I hear a deep southern drawl behind me asking if I could use a hand?

Now that is a nice sounding voice. I hate to turn around and ruin my immediate fantasy. Nice the few seconds it lasted, but I turn anyway.

Wow. A young Gary Cooper comes to mind. Okay, I love really old movies, go look him up on the internet. This was a dream cowboy come true. One tall, lean good looking cowboy complete with hat, standing right here, in my yard.

The hat is immediately taken off and he steps forward to introduce himself. "Grant Sheridan at your service, ma'am."

Wow, he even talks like the movies. Maybe this fantasy can last a little bit longer.

He is a special investigator from Texas, looking into the whereabouts of the widow of William

Garrison the Third. Personally, I hope I never see her again.

He asks if he can rent the cabin they had rented. Okay, I say sure and go get the paperwork and waivers. I ask if he has a sleeping bag and groceries. He does. Officers Reed and Porter have briefed him well.

We fill out all the paperwork and he pays for a week in advance. I show him to his new home for the week.

He is very good at getting every single piece of information I might possess out of me while helping me finish up the woodshed addition. I don't think Sheila sneezed while around me that he didn't know about by the time he finished. The same for Cary. I wasn't around McCready much, but told whatever I remembered about him, also. His search of the little cabin was total and complete. He cleaned it all up so well after he was done, that I doubt it has ever been quite that well done since it was built.

He really likes the place out here or is a very good actor. He can't get over how warm yet green it is. I think when he heard Alaska, he was thinking Frozen Cold North. It can be, just not usually in July.

It' a real shame this guy lives and works so far away. I would not mind getting better acquainted with him. He is nice, easy to be around and a good worker. We work on filling the new addition on the woodshed after we finish building it.

He asks about the guiding business and also the

taxidermy work I do in the winter. He thinks this is a pretty nice way to live. So do I.

We take a day off and go sight seeing and end up swimming at the hot springs. He was amazed by the Denali Park and we were lucky enough to actually see the mountain. Most people don't get to see it, even on sunny says. It makes it's own weather.

After he left for Texas, I actually missed him. It's not like there is phone service out here so I can call or for that matter, so he could call if he felt like it. Most people today can not understand the concept of no phone. They are dumbfounded by the no phone, no electricity, and no running water. Not even local mail delivery. For that matter, no matter what the ads say, no one delivers out here.

I get on with the business of making sure I have enough food and fuel on hand to make the winter. No matter that it is only the middle of the summer, winter looms. Winter is always in the back of my mind no matter what else is happening. Is there enough firewood? Is there going to be enough produce in my garden? Winter is almost like a presence, always there, hovering in the background.

There is last winter, this winter and next winter with brief appearances by very short summers in between. If you don't like winter, Interior Alaska is not for you.

Summers are short and with the daylight 24/7, a person tends to work until they have to eat or sleep. I find that I eat at very odd hours and sleep at even stranger hours. My watch quit sometime during hunting season and I don't really even know what day of the week or month it is. I have a clock in the house that tells what hour but not whether it is a.m. or p.m.

When Jim and Teri pull in, in Jim's old pickup, followed by Grant, in his, dressed in scruffy clothes, I am not sure if they are out for the fun of it or on a job. Teri laughs and says they are out checking, and they think maybe Cary and Sheila might still be in the area and they don't want to show up in a State Trooper vehicle. Must be why Grant had an older model pickup and dresses in cowboy gear.

Gee, that makes me feel like I have a target painted on my back and makes me nervous, just thinking those two might still be hanging around keeping an eye on what I am doing. So much for the peace and quiet of my own little piece of the wilderness.

They move back into their cabin and I start to feel like an undercover hangout for the police. With Grant staying in the cabin Cary and Sheila had used before and Jim and Teri staying in the other one fit for humans, I really didn't have another cabin to rent out. Hmmm, maybe we can renovate the third cabin while I have all this 'help' here.

We get right on it. Having something to do, keeps their minds off not catching the people they are looking for and takes my mind off maybe those same people keeping an eye on what I am doing. The cabin is small enough we manage to get in each other's way more than we get done, but somehow, it is soon looking pretty good. They load all the old junk and broken furniture in Jim's pickup. He will probably make it to town before I do. While putting the trash in his pickup, a small box falls out of a bag and I pick it up. It looks clean and not as old as all the junk we have been loading, so just because I am snoopy, I open it.

It is several different ID's, each with John McCready's picture on it but many different names on them. Okay, if Cary and Sheila each have the same thing, this could be a bit more difficult.

These are really good fake ID's. I would certainly think they were real. We move back into a cabin so we aren't standing out in the open and go through the little box. Each identity has everything from birth certificate to drivers license and passport. Not all are for the United States. Since we have handled the box before knowing what was in it, no telling who's fingerprints may be on it.

Jim sends Teri in with the box of ID's and his pickup. She will drop the load of trash for them to go through, also. Who knows, maybe they will find a clue in there. Better them than me.

We continue cleaning up the cabin and making it look livable. Grant has a knack for washing windows, they look really good when he is done, so he does them in all 3 cabins. He even offers to do them in my house. He actually enjoys it. Wow, and he looks good doing it, too. Forgive the drool, the man just looks so darn tempting.

Jim is trimming up the brush and small trees around the driveway and cabins and making the place look better than it ever has. He even cuts the lower limbs on the bigger trees, so it looks nice and open under the trees. Now it looks like there should be a couple of picnic tables out there.

About the time we decide to find something to fix for dinner, Teri is back. She even stopped at the truck stop and brought us dinner.

While we eat she tells us the folks in town were excited to see the little box, even though we had handled it. When she left, they were going through the rest of the trash with a fine toothed comb. She liked what the guys had done while she was gone.

While using the outhouse after dinner, I started wondering if maybe anything was stashed in it, so spent some time looking it all over. When I raised the entire seat, I found a large plastic bag taped to the underside of the boards. I motioned Teri over and she came in, wondering just what I wanted, I would think. Out here isn't like the movies where all the women troop to the bathroom together. I never could figure out why they traveled in packs or didn't they trust either the women in the group or their men to not make a play for the other while they were gone. Anyway, off track there, sorry.

Teri's eyes got big when she saw the taped bag. We left and sent the guys over to check it out.

While they are looking it over, a Trooper I don't now pulls in, in his State vehicle. Teri and I stand waiting for him to walk over to us. He looks all official and she steps aside with him a couple of moments, then points him to the outhouse.

Teri and I continue picking up branches the guys had cut and she tells me they must have found out something new or this guy wouldn't be here. He is Jeff Strickland and very good at his job, but not much sense of humor.

They remove the bag carefully while wearing gloves this time and we prepare another bag with papers in it and tape on the outside but leaving the top open, then push it down into the mess in the bottom of the outhouse. Teri is amazed, it is Jeff's idea. No sense of humor, huh?

They move the bugs over to the outhouse and set back up in Jim's cabin to listen. Yeah, I'm not using that one again, until they are gone.

Teri will move back in with me. Jeff is taking the new find back to town with him. Grant and Jim will share the other cabin and listening duties. Even without looking in the contents, we are pretty sure that bag was taped there by Cary or Sheila. Well, maybe by McCready, but his stuff was in the box, so probably not. Since they clam up every time I am too close, I probably will never know.

We finally decide we should get some sleep. The guys will sleep in shifts and we will hope if anyone comes messing around, that one of the guys hears them. Grant moves his stuff out of the first cabin and puts it in with Jim in the cabin they are now sharing. If Cary and Sheila come in like they did at my hunt camp, he doesn't want them going through his stuff.

Chapter 7

Teri and I go over to my house and get ready for bed. It has been a long busy day for both of us. I am just dozing off when I hear a gunshot. Teri heard it also. We get our clothes back on and get weapons before checking outside. I'm really glad it isn't dark at night, yet. Of course, anyone can see us coming, too, but somehow I feel more secure not going out in the dark looking around.

We separate, going through the trees on each side of the driveway out toward the cabins. I have a pistol in my waistband under my shirt but I am carrying the riot gun, Teri has her handgun out.

As we come around near the cabins, there is a crashing down through the trees to our left. Whoever or whatever is not trying to be quiet, just to leave.

Teri taps on the door as I stay back and on one side, not visible when the door opens. She calls out to Jim, but softly. He opens the door and pulls her inside, shutting the door. Hey, I'm still out here. I sit down against the side of the cabin, under a window. I can hear voices inside and it sounds like too many people. I edge around to the other side of the building, where I put a small trap door to pull a honey bucket out, in case I have clients that don't or won't use an outhouse. Lucky for me, that is not in use at present.

I carefully open the trap and slide myself into the small space. I pull the trap shut behind me. I ease over to the partly open door of the tiny bathroom. I do not recognize the man with his back to me. But I do recognize the looks on the faces of the police he has lined up in front of him while he gloats over having them where he wants them. I'm not sure what he will do if I say anything, so I just smash him over the head with a piece of 2 x 4 board that was left in the bathroom. He drops like a rock and Jim grabs his gun hand on the way down, so he doesn't shoot someone by accident.

We pull the curtains completely closed and latch the trapdoor I came in, from the inside, just in case. They have this guy trussed up like a present to themselves. He was looking for whatever was in the bag in the outhouse. First he trashed the other two cabins, looking for anything left in there. Then he came in here, intending on searching it also. The guys had acted dumb and not blown their cover and neither had Teri. The shot that woke us up, was the goon firing a warning shot at the guys or maybe he just missed and decided to go with it.

Evidently the crashing we heard outside was either a bear or a moose disturbed by us wandering around at night.

The guy don't show any signs of coming too any time soon, so we haul him out and load him in Jim's pickup. Jim has a large metal ring in the floor on the passenger side and he puts a chain through the restraints and down through the ring and locks the padlock. It is wrapped around the man's neck, arms and legs, so if he tries to kick or hit Jim, he will only damage himself. Then he heads for town with his load.

When Jim gets back, he tells me I should have smacked him a bit harder, he was pretty vile to listen to after he woke up. If half of what he threatened is for real, there are other folks after Cary and Sheila. Friends of John McCready. Seems he worked for two bosses and the dead one didn't know about the one now looking for Cary and Sheila. It is likely that even they don't now about this one.

Oh great, now I am going to have to watch out for guys with no neck, probably wearing suits, looking for clients I no longer have and who knows what they have or know about, that they will want. This doesn't look good for peace and quiet out here. I need a dog. I don't have a way to keep one around during hunting seasons when we are in more remote areas, living in a camp. I may just have to figure out a way to keep one in camp. A pet isn't disposable, they become part of the family and can't be ignored or mistreated. So if I get one, I have to plan ahead. It's like planning on having a child, to my way of thinking. Okay, so it is a big deal to me.

Teri and I go back to my house, and the men say they will get some sleep, but I don't think any of us get much sleep or rest, the rest of the night. We have cabins to clean again, tomorrow, or rather, later today.

W are a bleary eyed bunch the next day. Officer Strickland shows up the next day bright and early, well, before noon, and we are cleaning on the cabins. For someone without a sense of humor, he is getting a lot of fun out of this. Teri says she might have to rethink that no humor stuff. He even brought them a bag of fresh doughnuts which he hands over with a large smile. He even has a dimple.

He is supposed to patrol out this direction more often, and since there is only this one road, he pretty much is just going to be driving back and forth on it. I don't know why, but I feel better knowing he will be somewhere along this road. That makes no sense whatsoever, even to myself.

He sits on the pickup tailgate munching one of the doughnuts and talking to us while we work and soon he is down helping out, also. We soon have everything back in fairly good condition, but these cabins can't take a lot more of this treatment. I only expected them to withstand kids and pets, with an occasional fight, not for being torn apart in hiding things or searches for them .

I go fix some sandwiches and bring them over so we can all take a break. There is the remains of a cake hiding out in my kitchen, so I bring that, too. They have some sodas in the cabin they are staying in, so they add that to our meal.

Jeff has parked his vehicle over behind the storage shed and he is in the outhouse when a dark SUV pulls into my driveway. Grant is in the cabin, so it is just Jim, Teri and I outside when they stop right beside us.

Okay, these guys have no imagination. The two men inside the SUV look like clones of the jerk hauled in several hours ago. Big, beefy, no necks and wearing suits. They say they are looking for John McCready. I put on a sad face and tell them he is deceased, evidently drowned, in Fairbanks. They ask about his companions and I tell them I have not seen them. I only rent out cabins and once my clients are gone, I don't have any idea what or where they are doing or going. I complain about the last person in the cabin trashing the place and our having to completely redo it. That we have already hauled one full truck load to town.

They don't look happy that we have hauled trash to town. I didn't mention it was dropped at the Troopers headquarters. I always try to tell the truth, maybe just not the entire truth. I never had a good enough memory to actually lie, besides, it isn't a good idea to get in the habit, anyway.

They ask about renting a cabin and I tell them I don't think we have one ready yet for renting. Teri says she thinks we can have one ready in a couple of hours, if they are not in a hurry for it. Thanks, Teri. I'm trying to get rid of them and you want them around?

They grumble and drive off. They promise they will be back. Not what I wanted to hear.

"Really? You want them back here? I could have done without ever seeing or hearing from any of them ever again." I sorta yell.

The guys are busy bugging the end cabin yet again. They will leave the set up in the outhouse and have a second one for the cabin. Jim, Jeff, Grant and Teri all are working hard to get the cabin ready and the bugs in place. I am less enthusiastic.

Jeff has to leave soon, so he tells them he will go off shift and change and come back out to help them. He will be in his old vehicle and ready to work. I'm still wondering what our uninvited guest was driving and where is his vehicle? I mention this to them before Jeff leaves. He says he will check all the gravel pits and side roads on his way back, within walking distance. There aren't many.

When Jeff comes back later that evening, he is driving an ancient Jeep. It looks like a relic from WWll. The motor sounds like it would do well on a racetrack. He says he located a car, parked near the old bridge, and evidently last night's visitor had a partner and someone didn't like him much. He was dead, in the car. Preliminary investigation looks like he was shot while sitting in the car with his window down. Looks like a rifle was used. I tell them Cary used a Contender handgun with a 308 barrel for his bear hunt. Jim and Jeff both perk up at that.

Teri and I go on over to the house. The guys can sort out how they are spending the night and the

SUV hasn't made it back looking for a cabin for the night. I leave the paperwork with Jim to make them sign if they show up.

We actually get a good night's sleep. We even manage to oversleep. The guys finally come banging on the front door to see if we are okay. Teri stumbles out to let them in and then we get dressed and I prepare breakfast for us all. The bread left over from hunt camp makes fine French toast and the leftover egg mixture and the rest of the bread go into a bread pudding for dessert later this evening.

Instead of walking back to the cabins in a group, everyone goes out the door at intervals and walks either through the woods where they can observe the cabin area a while before going on, or around and circle the entire area and come back in on the driveway. I do my chores around the yard and house before I go out to see what is happening. A nice quiet day would be nice. I wouldn't mind a nice quiet year or two, even.

I get my wish for the day. Very quiet. I went back to my house and worked in the garden all afternoon. It needed the weeding, badly. The greenhouse was looking like a jungle. By the time I was done for the day, I felt like I had been run over by a truck. I am used to working, but it has been a while since I have done this much weeding in one day.

The pot of stew is done and the pudding cooled The pan of yeast rolls are ready to come out of the oven. The officers have decided not to leave the cabin totally unattended from now on. So they will only come over one at a time or bring things back so the others don't have to leave their post. Jim comes over and I send dinner back with him in a huge box. Teri will come back as soon as he reaches the cabin.

She is tired when she reaches my house. We eat and she almost falls asleep at the table so I tell her to go on in, her bed is waiting. I wash up the dishes and check the doors and windows and I soon am heading for my bed, also. For some reason, I put the alarm under the edge of the front door again before going to bed. We are both jolted out of sleep a few hours later by it's shrieking. We both come out of our beds with guns ready and check around the edge of the door frame. We have taken to sleeping fairly well fully dressed, so we aren't fumbling around for clothes, although my foot is feeling around for a slipper.

I'm not gung-ho on going on out to see what triggered the alarm. It certainly didn't go off on it's own. Teri is slowly easing her way into the living room. I go around the other edge of the room and we both check out the windows on each side of the door.

As I get near the door, I hear someone whispering loudly, "Kelly? Are you in there, Kelly?"

I can't tell if it is a male or female voice. I'm not real sure I want to answer it, either. Finally Teri whispers back, "What do you want? Who is it?"

An immediate shot right through the door, just under the peep hole, is her answer. Now that is downright unfriendly. I pull up the riot gun and let loose also right through my door at the same level as the shot came in. Yeah, going to have to replace that door.

We are both unharmed, but by the sounds on my porch, someone else has been harmed. By the sounds, quite badly. We wait a bit.

I see the flicker of movement out in the trees and watch a bit. It is Grant, so I figure at least one of the others will be somewhere on their way to my house, also. My ears are still ringing, a 12 gauge in the house, is bad enough, but fired 3 times, not good at all. I have it reloaded, but really don't want to shoot it in the house again.

Teri was smart enough to put something in her ears when she saw me raise the riot gun. She motions that someone is coming up onto the porch. I peek from the side out through the huge hole in my door and see Grant pulling Sheila away from the door and down the steps of the porch. She don't look too good. He is staunching the flow of blood out of her shoulder and arm. My porch is going to require some deep cleaning. She comes to and tells him Cary held her in front of him when he shot through the door to start with. What a gentleman. Let the lady go first.

Teri and I will haul her sorry butt in to the hospital. She will be okay, just not apt to be using that arm for a long time and only after a lot of therapy. She does say a few pellets hit Cary, just not many and not in areas to incapacitate him at all. With any luck, maybe he will get infected.

Teri reads her her Rights and turns on a recorder, just in case she feels like sharing, on the way to town.

Surprisingly enough, she does share quite a bit. She says she doesn't know what is going on, first McCready was with them, then he was missing, then he was floating, and they were on the run out here in the middle of nowhere with not many roads to chose from to get anywhere else. She says Cary is crazy and she doesn't now what his problem is. According to her, he was always just her older stepbrother that she adored and he always fixed all her problems. So she ran to him first, when her marriage was going to pot.

Everything just seemed to go downhill faster after that. She had been in love and signed the prenup The Third pushed under her nose before their wedding. If she was still with him after 5 years, she would get a large allowance increase. After 10 years, another allowance increase. If she left, for any reason, before 5 years, she would get nothing. Their 5th Anniversary was coming up and he started smacking her around. She was bound and determined to stay, but it kept getting worse and worse.

I didn't know how much to believe. I did see all the bruises and they did look like they were given at different times by the colors and fading. If she was lying, she was darn good at it. She was in a lot of pain and we had not given her anything for it. It was almost like she was talking to keep her mind off her pain. Luckily for her, the door had absorbed a lot of the force and power of the birdshot and they were getting out of the way by the second and third shot. She is lucky I wasn't using slugs or double ought. Okay, I could probably have stopped at one shot.

Teri is on her cell phone as soon as we are in range to find out where to deliver Sheila. An on duty Trooper will meet us at the hospital and take over from there.

Chapter 8

After we drop off Sheila, we go do a bit of grocery shopping. Then fuel up the pickup and head back home. On our way out, there is a vehicle dogging our tail. We are still in cell range so Teri calls it in. We slow down a bit and are surprised to hear a chopper overhead. They were in the area and answered her call. Just before the SUV following us notices the chopper, the passenger opens fire on us. The people in the helicopter notice immediately and return fire which scares the peewadden out of the driver or he is hit, and they go right on off the side in a really good curve in the road.

We stop and the chopper lands. I am supposed to stay back, but I walk over to the side and still have my trusty riot gun in my hands when the passenger sneaks up through the bushes and starts to aim at the pilot. I am right behind him and mutter don't even think about it, and he starts to swing toward me, I clock him in the side of the head with the shotgun. Oh yeah, it is one of the guys from the SUV that wanted to rent a cabin and was looking for

McCready. The other is still in the SUV.

I knew I was going to hear about not staying in the vehicle, I am a civilian and all that, but dang, I just saved the pilot from getting shot. Teri finally says thanks. The other two look at her odd. She shrugs and says "Well, she did just save you."

Then the pilot mumbles out a thanks and we head back for the pickup and continue on our trip to my place. I ask her if I should have just let the guy shoot the pilot? She says no, when they have time to think it over, they may realize I did them a favor. She asks me if I ever considered becoming a police officer. I tell her, "No, for the same reason I didn't become a school teacher. Not allowed to use force to keep order."

She is not sure whether or not I am joking. I am, but I just smile when she asks. She does say I have a way with a weapon. It's just that I don't like getting hurt. She says she don't either, but they have to follow protocol. See? That's what I mean.

We make it home without any more people shooting at us. Teri tells the guys what all has happened since we left and they tell her the guys in the SUV had actually stopped and rented the cabin for tonight, just after we left. They asked about us, and not even thinking, Jim says we went to town. They left soon after. I will not be giving them back their deposit.

We go check out the cabin and they actually left some stuff in the cabin, but now I am a little jumpy and wonder if it is going to go boom if we move any of it. The others look at each other like the random thought hadn't crossed their minds. Now they are jumpy, too.

We pile a bunch of old quilts and an old mattress we forgot to haul to the dump over their gear and yank the quilt off the bed with all that on it. There is a muffled whump and we are knocked down, but nothing major.

I start to reach for it and Grant pulls me back. Sure enough, there is a second muffled whump. Well, if I had just came in and grabbed their stuff off the bed, I would now be in bitty pieces around the room. Not the way I want to lose weight.

We clear the shredded mattress and quilts and what's left of their luggage out of the cabin and right into the back of Jeff's pickup. He has to go back to town and his regular job. He is giving them more to sort through in town. Maybe they can find out where the explosives came from, anyway. They will start hating to see any vehicle pull in from out here.

I won't have any old junk laying around out here by the end of the summer, at this rate. This has been a too much crap, not enough shovels kind of day. I hope the rest of it is boring as can be. There is a lot to be said for boring.

After Jeff leaves, we finish cleaning up the cabin and have it looking pretty good in case someone else actually wants to rent to poor thing. I'm amazed the windows are intact. At least we had the door open. My ears aren't as messed up as they were from the shotgun earlier, anyway.

The guys replaced my shredded front door with the salvaged door I had leaned against the back of the house. I was considering adding another door back there, but that can wait.

I finally get the groceries unloaded and put them away. Then I prepare something for dinner. Grant comes over and offers to help. He is actually nice to work around. I could get used to this, but he lives in Texas and I would melt there.

While we are setting the table, he mentions that he has decided to move to Alaska. Huh? Can he read minds or is mine transparent?

He continues talking and tells me he has been up several times before, but it was always winter. He enjoyed the winters but wasn't sure how he would like summers here.

Okay, that is different. Usually people come up here in the summer and decide to stay and then can't handle the winters.

He says he volunteered on the Iditarod Dog Race and then on the Yukon Quest Race which is even harder and during colder months of the winter. He was located in one of the remote cabins on the long stretch between Dawson, YT. and Circle, Alaska. He said that was one of the best times he ever had and he loved going cross country to get there on a snow machine.

Hmmm, maybe he would enjoy living up here, if he has already done all of that and loved it. We continue talking and he asks about how I spend my winters.

I tell him I do the taxidermy work on the bears my spring clients take and contract me for. I do some painting and a bit of writing, but nothing much. I start cutting firewood for the next winter, very early, before the sap starts coming up. Before the bears come out, I set up my areas I will be hunting in, and also sometimes if I have time, I tap some birch trees for sap to make syrup.

He is interested in all of it. He says he would like to take a year off and just do what I do, if possible. Do I ever rent out a cabin by the year?

Wow, wasn't expecting that. I'm not sure how winter worthy any of those cabins are. They were built for hunters in the spring and fall and an occasional guest during the summer. I guess if he is serious, he could upgrade one a bit and make it more winter worthy. They only have single pane windows, so that would be the first thing to fix and a better heater would be second. Then a really good supply of firewood would need to be cut.

I tell him if he wants to do all of that, he can use the cabin. He says I need to make some actual cash off the deal too, so says he will fix up the cabin and pay me rent. How can I refuse this deal? Not even going to try.

We pack dinner for Grant and Jim in a basket, and he carries it over and Teri comes back to have dinner with me. We do up the dishes and she wants to talk about Grant staying out here for the winter. Teri asks if I would prefer she stay over with Jim and have Grant stay here with me. I decline.

We start in the next day, going over the cabin Jim and Grant are staying in, to see what would be needed to make it winter worthy. It is the only one of the 3 that is insulated. It doesn't have much and needs a better vapor barrier. A thermal break of foil faced foam board inside the insulation but before the vapor barrier would work even better. I mention that and the Alaskans agree. Grant figures we know what we are talking about. Then he asks if it wouldn't be better to just start insulating from scratch on one of the other cabins, since this one is, a little bit already but needs more. That way they could continue living in this one while renovating one of the others. Sounds okay to me.

Hi picks the middle one. It hasn't been bugged, shot at or blown up any and since we cleaned it up a while back, it looks pretty good. It is small enough to heat easily and has enough room for one person to be quite comfortable for a long time or several on short term camping trip. He can take out the extra set of bunk beds and have more room.

We measure the cabin and the windows, even the door. He asks if there is anything any of us want from town and heads in to pick up supplies. When he makes up his mind, he gets right on it.

While he is gone, we pull off the plywood I have used for paneling inside the cabin. We pull nails and stack the panels against the side of the house, in the order we took them off. Depending on what he does about windows and stuff, maybe we can just slap them back on. Would sure save time.

He is back by the time we get done with our late lunch. It wasn't much of a lunch and that is a good thing, since he stopped at the truck stop and brought pie. We may not need dinner after that.

Then we all unload his pickup and start right in on insulating. He bought replacement windows the same size as the single pane windows in the cabin, so it is easy to remove and replace. By evening, we have made a lot of progress. Windows changed out and the ceiling insulated, thermal break taped in place and vapor barrier over it all. Tomorrow, we should have it almost finished. I'm impressed.

Grant also has some stuff just needing heated up from the truck stop, for our dinner, so it is an easy meal to fix, tonight.

The guys wake up to someone rummaging around in the outhouse and then cursing when they see the corner of the plastic bag down in the mess at the bottom. The recorder is on and this should make the top 10 in police circles for entertaining listening. Someone really is not happy and very vocal about it. Soon the sound of retching can be heard and another voice speaks up about not getting any on him.

Grant and Jim have dressed and snuck out of the cabin and over by the outhouse, one on each side. The two men coming out of the outhouse are complaining and talking about how unhappy someone is going to be about the condition of the bag's contents. Grant tells them to halt and hands on top their heads, they, of course, bolt right into Jim. The clean one in the lead slams right into Jim and the filthy, slimy one smacks into him with the soggy bag of papers. The clean one starts screaming about him getting all that mess on him and the other one is complaining about watching where he was going and no sudden stops if he didn't want to get himself dirty. Grant restrains them and fastens a chain between the hands behind their backs and the leg restraints, then loops them together.

Whoever is sending these goons out here must have an unlimited supply. They all look alike. Big, beefy and no neck, in suits. I don't think anyone is going to want to clean these two's suits after tonight.

They have the standard dark SUV parked just out of sight of the cabins. Jim searchs the SUV very well and especially the backseat area. No one wants to haul the smelly catch in to town in their own vehicle, so they put them in the backseat of their own SUV and Jim will drive it while Grant follows in his pickup. They read them their Rights and leave the recorder on, for the trip to town.

Either the goons didn't see where the recorder was put, or forgot about it, as they did speak quite a bit, very low, in the backseat and the recorder caught every word. It was too low for Jim to hear, but when the volume is turned up, it is very easy to hear everything they are saying. Someone in town is going to be very pleased to get that recording.

By the time the men get back, the next morning, Teri and I have been working on the cabin quite a while. We have most of the insulation in the walls and over half of the foam board up and taped. Once the guys pitch in, we have that finished and the vapor barrier up and taped. The plywood goes back on easily Looks like my renter can move in, any time. I do tell him he might want to pick up some propane lights and copper tubing and set the cabin up for lights soon. He asks about putting the holes through the wall and when I tell him I used the 44 mag to drill mine, he sputters and laughs.

It works better than a drill which catches in the insulation and pulls it around the bit tearing it loose and making hollow areas in the wall. Just make sure what is on the other side before doing it. He still thinks I am joking, Teri and Jim just grin.

We start adding finishing touches to make the cabin more comfortable for the winter. He needs some sort of stove to cook on, preferably propane although some people rough it with a camp stove. It's getting very hard to find a propane stove that does not need electricity to function which sort of ruins the whole concept of having a propane stove.

I have an old 1950 propane cook stove that uses a match to light. I'm going to have a rough time if that stove ever totally quits. I tell Grant his best bet is a used stove.

Chapter 9

After a couple of days with no one showing up, either we start to get complaisant or just plain aren't paying attention, but one day when Teri and I go in the house after working a while in the garden, there sits Cary, in my living room.

He asks how Sheila is. I haven't heard, but she is either still in Fairbanks or headed to Texas. Since he was holding her in front of him at the time, I find his concern a bit suspect. However, he is favoring his own shoulder a bit, so maybe a few pellets did connect. I hope.

I ask him why he shot through my door. He doesn't seem to remember it but keeps telling us to take care of Sheila, she didn't know what was going on. I told him I didn't know what was going on either. He says it was all McCready's getting greedy that led to all the trouble. He is waving that gun around and starting to look a bit more scary.

He isn't looking too good and when Teri moves over to the other side of him, he doesn't even notice. She picks up the first thing her hand touches, which is a crescent wrench I had used earlier to change a propane bottle and had not put back. I hope she don't use full swing, or we will be cleaning house this evening.

She swings it none too gently and connects with a satisfying thud against the back of his head. He folds up without a sound. I'm not sure whether or not she would get in trouble for smacking him like that so offer to take the blame for it, they expect stuff like that from me. She refuses. She says it could get addictive, so she will have to refrain in the future but since he had a gun on me, she didn't want to just say hands up. She may get talked to about using force, but they will understand the circumstances.

She put restraints on him and it looks like someone else may have been shooting at him also as he has a larger hole in his shoulder than what he would have from just the few pellets that missed Sheila.

It looks slightly infected, so we clean it out some while he is still out and pour on some antiseptic gunk I have under the sink. He is running a bit of fever with it, too. She loosely covers it and goes to see who wants to haul him to town. I know they will be thrilled with yet another trip in.

Jim drives over. He and Grant bundle Cary into the small backseat and fasten him to the floor. I doubt if he is going to feel much like trying anything, but better safe than sorry. Grant is staying, Jim will take Cary in. Seems like we are giving the hospital quite a bit of business from out here, also. Not even much mess to clean up in the house or repairs to make. We must be getting better at this.

Sheila is still in the hospital in Fairbanks and is not wanted in Texas at the present. She has a very good alibi for her husband's time of death. She was getting some kind of award for some charitable works when he died. Her picture was in the newspapers at the time. McCready was her escort and Cary was in San Francisco on layover, waiting for his flight on up to Alaska.

I still can't figure out why so many people are trying to find them. There has to be money involved or power. Cary said McCready got greedy, but for what?

Jim gets back, late, and shares nothing where I can hear it. Dang, what good is it to be right in the middle of everything if I am left in the dark? I try to get information out of Teri when she comes back over, but she won't tell, either. I even try bribing her with a batch of fudge. She doesn't give in. She has will power.

So I maybe pout just a little bit, but the fudge is really good and soon get over it and read a bit before going to bed. Chocolate fixes everything.

I actually get a good full night's sleep. It seems like a very long time since that has happened. During spring bear hunts, we mostly hunt at night. Then this year, there have been all the fun and games with Cary and Sheila. Before the hunts, it was winter and I have to keep checking the fire once in a while so the house doesn't freeze up. Me too, of course. Usually between spring bear hunts and fall moose and bear hunts, I actually get to have some full night's of sleep. Just not this year. I miss them.

We get back to work on the cabin Grant is planning on spending the winter in. He won't have any electricity unless he wants to go buy himself a generator and go from there. The cabin is not wired, so he would have to also use extension cords and power strips. It can get expensive pretty fast. He did find some nice propane lights to hang on the walls and runs the copper tubing around hooking them up. The place will look really good by the time he finishes fixing it up. I will have to fix the other two just so they don't look bad by comparison.

By evening, we have the cabin in good condition to live in year around. I really had considered doing this, but never seemed to have time or money to actually do it. The stove I have in there is small, so he will probably need to get a larger one that he won't have to feed every couple of hours. He thinks he can make do.

One of the neighbors is selling cut firewood, so he buys several cord and the man delivers it. We stack it, then tarp it, so it doesn't get wet or loaded with snow before he uses it. Too bad we don't have time or materials to build some kind of woodshed over it.

I wake up to the sound of hammers the next morning and wonder what I forgot. When I finally make it over to the cabins, they have the framework up for a woodshed of sorts over the firewood stack. It is entirely built of poles, so nails are the only supplies they have needed. They even placed a solid roof of poles with a tarp stretched over, to shed rain and probably be okay on shedding snow, also. Nice. Later, it could be used as a picnic area for people staying in the cabins. I could put an actual roof on it someday, too. Maybe half walls of poles and screen the upper half for picnickers. This is really great. I go make a large batch of homemade bread as a treat for them.

The smell of the baking bread must have reached them or they have perfect timing. I am just taking the pan of stuffed hot rolls out of the oven as they come in the front door. I figured these would be better than just making sandwiches. I filled them with potatoes, sausage and onion filling and a slice of cheese to hold the filling together.

They must like them or are extremely hungry as they each eat 2 and split another one between the guys. I am amazed they could still move after eating. These are some very large filled rolls. I can never eat more than one.

Everyone is moving much slower after lunch, but we all go back over to finish up the job on the woodshed. I can't get over how nice it is and how handy it will be later, for guests. I should have done it years ago.

When the guys go in the cabin to check on something, I think I should check for blueberries. Teri comes along and we find enough ripe ones to make some dumplings for dessert tonight. She says she will have to work out to keep from gaining too much to fit into her uniform, staying out here. She is such a slender woman, I don't think she has to worry. We take our find to the house and I clean them. Our wild blueberries are so strong flavored, I can add quit a bit of water to them and still have lots of flavor. So I mix them with sugar and cornstarch, add the water and put on the stove. While they are cooking, I mix the dough for dumplings.

I have just dropped in the dumplings and trying to think of something to fix for dinner when the guys show up. They say all they want is more of lunch, until they smell the dumplings.

I take them at their word and put the leftover rolls in the oven to reheat. Between the smell of the rolls heating in the oven and the dumplings on top the stove, they are practically salivating by the time the rolls are hot. I have a green salad made to have with the rolls for dinner, so it has a little bit of healthy food included. Nobody complains and I don't think it is ALL because of the sign in the kitchen. "The First Person To Complain Is The Next Cook." That sign saves listening to a lot of complaints.

The guys volunteer to go pick blueberries the next day. They really liked the dumplings. They figure they are going to get pulled off this stakeout soon and want to get lots of blueberry treats before they have to go.

While they are gone berry picking, someone tears apart the outhouse and the cabin Cary, Sheila and

McCready had stayed in. The sound activated bugs catch the whole thing. Someone is really upset about something but for the life of me, I can't figure out what they think they will find after all that has already happened to those places. So many people have already looked them over and checked everything, there can't be any place that hasn't been searched already. The other 2 cabins weren't touched. Maybe it is because of all the obvious work being done on them or do the searchers really have an area that whatever it is, is supposed to be in?

The officers dust everything for prints, then they repair the outhouse. Those used to be called the "necessary" for a reason.

Once they have it repaired, they replace the lost bug in it. Teri and I continue to use the one over by my house. There is only so much I am willing to share.

Grant says they have the best motive for trashing the place, it keeps them here and they like it out here. Everyone else goes, "Shhhhhhhh, not out loud."

Officer Strickland stops by to see how we are getting along. He talks to Grant and Jim while they are finishing up the repairs and cleaning out the cabin. He says he wouldn't mind coming back out and staying on his days off. He likes it out here. He is turning out to be a lot nicer and easier to work with, than I expected to start with. It's fine with me if it is okay with the others.

The Troopers are really going above and beyond

on what they need to do to be undercover here and are helping me out an incredible amount. I could never afford to pay for having all the work done that they are doing. Having Jeff come out and work once in a while is more than okay.

While using the outhouse by my house, I notice that board near the door is loose again. I have fixed it so many times, I am tired of it. I grab a screw gun and fasten it down with screws. Maybe that will finally hold it. Maintenance has fallen behind. I've got to get things taken care of better, around here. I really need to hire an assistant for the hunts, that would help out a lot. All the free help I am getting now is wonderful, but I can't really ask them to do regular maintenance. They are just supposed to keep an eye on the cabin area.

Chapter 10

Tonight, I start a list of all I need to get done before the fall hunts start. I am booked solid for moose. While I am working on it, Grant comes in and asks what would he need to do to qualify as an Assistant Guide?

I better look that up to be sure. It's been a while since I even had to remember any of this. I do know that for a nonresident, it is a lot more expensive. He says that is not a problem. All I know for sure is that a person has to work as a Class A Assistant Guide 3 years before being qualified to even apply to take the test to be a Registered Guide.

I know he is over 18 years old, which is the first thing they ask. But he hasn't hunted in the State for 30 days in two different years, I don't think. I will have to ask him. Being an Officer of the Law, he must already have a First Aid card. I would write a letter of recommendation and intent to employ. That should cover his requirements, and it is $600 for a nonresident Assistant Guide license.

I ask him about the hunting in the State requirement, and he says no, he hasn't. That lets him out of being an Assistant Guide for a couple of years until he gets experience, anyway. By the time he qualified on that, he would be a resident and the license would be almost half price. That is, if he plans on staying in Alaska.

At dinner that evening, Jeff is back and when we start talking about guiding, he says he already has his Class A Assistant Guide license. He has already put in for hunting season off. He wants to guide after he gets out of the Troopers.

Jeff and Grant both volunteer to help out during hunting season. Wow, from no help at all to two nice men. One can even take out clients. I shouldn't have any trouble with either of them skirting around the game laws to satisfy a client, either. Wohoo.

That has always been one of my worries, about hiring Assistants. I am liable for everything they do, in the field. If one of them allows an illegal animal to be shot, I pay for it, usually by losing my license. That license was too hard to get, for me to do something that might put it at risk.

We talk about guiding all evening. Even Teri is interested in it. We discuss the pros and cons on bear baiting. I used to be against it. Now I see that it keeps people from shooting immature bears or sows with cubs, if the hunter is an ethical hunter. There are always the exceptions. Luckily, they are few and far between. Not sure why I had to get one, this year. Special, I guess.

Chapter 11

Someone tried to either abduct or kill Sheila in the hospital in town. She was healing up fairly well, and they were considering sending her back to Texas to recover. Now she is in a coma and no one knows just what happened, entirely.

The hospital and the police are still trying to figure out how the attempt was made and what the outcome was supposed to be. Someone had managed to drug Sheila and was taking her out in a wheelchair. As they went by Cary's room, his guard was talking to him and they saw Sheila being wheeled by.

Cary asked what was happening and the person wheeling the chair panicked and tried to run down the hall pushing the wheelchair. They collided with the food cart coming off the service elevator and threw Sheila headfirst into the metal doors which were closing. She hit wrong and somehow managed to fracture a bone in her neck. Between the drug and the injury, she has not regained consciousness. The person wheeling her chair has not been caught and they are not certain whether it was a slender male or a tall female.

An attempt was made on Cary, later, but he is kind

of guarded. The guard had gone to the bathroom and came back to see someone injecting something into Cary's IV. He thinks it was the same person. He pulled the IV line loose and called security downstairs to see if they can find the person on any of the tapes. He was afraid to pursue the person at the time, not knowing if any of the injected material would make it into Cary's vein.

The hospital is not too happy with the folks being sent in from out here. Security has been beefed up a lot. I'm not that happy about these folks, either. Yes, because of them, I am getting lots of work done on my place   But, because of them, I need more work done on my place. This definitely isn't the type of publicity I want or need for my business.

That night while we are getting ready for bed, Teri and I somehow get on the topic of marriage. She has been married twice and thinks she may not have a very good job for domestic bliss. She and Jim have been edging around the subject of maybe dating. He hasn't had very good luck in his relationships, either. I tell her I was married once, for a few minutes. At the reception, after the wedding, I caught my new groom kissing my former best friend in the hallway, near the coat rack. The only good thing I can think of out of that mess, is, at least I didn't find out after we had kids   I would like to have a family, but the prospects are not looking good. I am not going to just settle, I want the real deal.   Currently, I figure my Prince Charming took a wrong turn somewhere, got lost and is too stubborn and stupid to ask for directions.

When we get around the next day, we decide to pick berries in earnest. Teri and I will go to the flats up overlooking the Tanana Valley. The plants are small but they usually are loaded with nice large blueberries. I grab 2 milk crates for us to sit on, so we don't cripple ourselves bending over picking berries from ankle high bushes. We take a couple of berry pickers with us. The berries will need more cleaning than if picked by hand, but we will have more, usually.

I put a roast on to slow bake in the oven while we are gone. I load up the roaster pan with a lot of assorted vegetables to cook right along with it.

We find a very good patch of berries right after we drive over Ptarmigan Pass. The bushes are blue from the road. We pack some containers, our berry pickers and the milk crates over to the edge of the patch and immediately start picking. I have an old towel in the backseat of my pickup and more containers. The wild berries are very juicy, so when we get some in our containers, we go to the pickup, and pour the berries down the towel into another container. Most of the leaves and twigs stick to the towel.

By the time we clean out this small patch, we are both ready to quit. I think we have more than 5 gallons of berries. I want to dry some to use in cookies and muffins, can some for pies and make some liqueur.

When we walk in the house, the roast smells very

good. We are more than ready for dinner. I fix a loaf of garlic bread to put in the oven with the roast for the last half hour, after pouring off some of the pan juices to make brown gravy.

The smells from the kitchen must be wafting their way to the cabins, as the men show up soon after and are ready to eat. They are impressed by the containers of berries lined up on the counters. Two of the men are familiar with the area we picked in and know how short those bushes are.

When I take dinner out of the oven, I have trays of berries ready to go in, to dry. Might as well use the heat while it lasts. I'll start a canner of berries after dinner.

Teri does the dishes while I start the canner of berries. She watches what I am doing and so do the men. She said her grandmother used to can, but her mother never did.

I soon have 3 canners going on the stove and a couple more trays drying in the oven. I happen to have some 180 proof in my pantry and start a batch of liqueur. Eyes are bugging out around the table when they see what I put in it. That will get finished tomorrow evening. I also make the syrup that has to be added, after it is strained.

The motion activated cameras we have placed around the cabins have some interesting pictures of our vandals or whatever they are. One shows the license plate very well for the vehicle used. Jeff will take it with him when he goes in tomorrow. He will take all the photos in, and maybe with the recordings they have, someone will recognize one or both of the men responsible. They are not trashing the place as much, now, but they are still doing a systematic search.

I would like to know how they are managing to keep us under surveillance so easily without us seeing any sign of them. So I start a systematic search to see if we are being bugged, also. They would have to be staying somewhere fairly close to pick up anything, I think. So I am thinking maybe I can find where they are either staying or where they have some sort of recorder system.

Teri and I start checking all the berry patches near the edges of my property and looking for sign of anyone being around. On the second day, we find sign of someone using a trail to and from the road, going up the hill just across the highway from my place. There is no private property on that side of the road, so we go back and tell the guys.

When the men go to investigate, Teri and I station ourselves in the trees and brush on my side of the road, where we are not easily seen. We have a couple of cameras and Teri has a video camera, also. She has the camera set on a tripod and has a remote to turn it on.

As Jim and Grant go up parallel to the trail I had found, Teri and I heard someone coming down the hill through the brush even farther from the old trail than Jim and Grant were going. We moved down to intercept them as they reached the roadway. We find a dark pickup parked backed into the brush on my property, just off the highway, but not visible from the road. Teri quickly snaps photos of the license plates and truck and I am trying to make sure the pickup won't start. I don't have time, so just stab my knife into the bottom radiator hose and slash for all I am worth. They can start it, but if we watch which way they go, we should find them along the road fairly soon.

We scoot back into the brush and sit still as they come across the road to the pickup and jump in. She had the video camera going from the time they came into view and I was busy stabbing hoses.

They are leaving a trail of radiator fluid from the time they pull out, so we hurry back to the house and get Jim's pickup. He and Grant are coming out of the brush when we reach the driveway, so I walk back to the house and Teri goes with them, taking the cameras.

Jeff pulls in on patrol a short while after they leave, checking to see how we are doing. I tell him what has just happened and he leaves to see if he can catch up to them. If he can, maybe they won't have to be anything but concerned citizens helping out a stranded motorist and not let on they are all police.

As he heads on toward town, I go back inside. I am fairly certain no one has been in my house to plant anything, but the rest of the place is usually not locked up. I grab my tool belt and stick my handgun down in the nail pouch. I put a smaller one in my bra. I have an odd little knife in my boot.

Maybe I am just a wee bit paranoid. But since 'they' really do seem to be out to get me, is it still paranoia?

So I search and do some small repairs. While I am up on a ladder, reaching into a small space under the eaves on one of the little cabins, a soft voice behind me suggests I not turn around, just back down the ladder and I won't be hurt. Dang, I just can't get the hang of following orders, even softly spoken orders.

I whirl around on the stepladder and have pulled the gun out of the nail pouch and shot the guy reaching for me as I turn. He falls into the ladder and I fall off the ladder, landing on top of him and shooting the other guy that has a grip on a pale, ill looking Cary. Since I didn't really mean to shoot that one as I hadn't even seen him yet, I don't do a very good job of it.

They both fall, also, as Cary couldn't hardly stand on his own and the other guy is shot in the belly. Ouch, that's gotta hurt. This one I am sitting on at least broke my fall, and my fall may have broken his neck against the ladder leg. At this point, I am thinking better him than me.

I manage to get off the one I'm sitting on and grab Cary away from the other guy. The other guy is really in pain and he is also very angry and is trying to get his gun aimed at me enough to let me join him in his pain. Since I am not particularly pleased with Cary, I yank him between me and the other guy and Cary does manage to slap the gun aside as he crashes into the man. Cary gives me a sickly grin and passes out.

I make sure the gun is in my possession and search both men for any other weapons before checking on Cary and what condition the other two are in. It can't be too good.

Cary is still out and I straighten him out a bit and raise his feet. Then I check the one by the ladder and he is not ever going to be a problem again. Last is the guy cussing over in a heap near Cary. When I lean down to check on him, he tries to grab my gun so I kick him under the jaw. Now he is nice and quiet while I straighten him out a bit and check to see how much damage he has. He has the bullet hole going in, but no exit hole, so it is still wandering around somewhere in there.

I do find a hide out gun in his belt buckle. I pull the whole thing off and stash it over on one side. Then I go recheck the one by the ladder. He has one of those cute belt buckle guns also, so I pull it off, too. Hey, he might be playing possum and use it if I leave it on him. Yeah, keep telling myself that.

I put the ladder back upright and go check out the place I was trying to check when so rudely interrupted. Well, actually, he was rather polite when he interrupted.

When I reach into the little space, I feel a plastic bag and pull it out carefully. It is a handgun in the bag, with some kind of note. I push it back in place and wish I was wearing gloves.

I hear a vehicle pulling in as I am coming down

the ladder. Not knowing who it is, I am a little jumpy, so I duck in behind the closest tree and wait. Somehow, my gun is in my hand. I might even be shaking just a little bit.

I am so relieved to hear Teri and Jim laughing as they walk over, that I stand up too fast and almost pass out. They see me stumble and then they spot the extras, laying around. Cary is starting to come to and the one near him is still mumbling curses that they can hear now that they are closer. Since the third one isn't making any noise, they almost trip over him.

As they look around and I am the only one standing, they are speechless. "Three? You took out three?" Teri squeaks out.

"No, Cary don't count. He was evidently their prisoner. Although he hasn't been able to talk, so not sure what is wrong with him. He looks like they worked him over pretty good, though. I did pick up a couple of small souvenirs from the other two, can I keep them, please?"

I do hand over the usual weapons they had on them, handguns and knives, even a pair of knuckles, but still haven't pulled out the belt buckle guns. I tell them about the gun up under the eaves in a plastic bag. They look at each other, he pulls on a pair of gloves and heads up the ladder.

He finds the gun and brings it down. Teri blurts out, "Is that the one they are looking for in Texas?"

Okay, so maybe this is the weapon that killed William Garrison The Third. She winks at me, so I know that is the only way she could have let me know a little bit of what is happening in the Texas investigation. Jim isn't too happy, but he gives a little grin. If I hadn't of been so snoopy, it would probably never have been found. Cary must have known where it was and they were coming to retrieve it. Heck, Cary probably put it there.

While we are watching Jim retrieve the gun and we are looking at it, Cary manages to disappear. I knew I should have just tied him up. I was positive he was too injured to move, let alone get away. I hate being wrong.

The other man is still mumbling, but now he has a knife sticking out of him. Okay, so I didn't search Cary. How did he manage to get a knife, anyway? Or did someone else stick the knife in the goon and help Cary get away? For living out in the middle of nowhere, there are a lot of unexplained folks running around out here.

I ask Teri and Jim how it went on the chase for the men up on the hill. They caught up with the pickup a few miles down the road. It overheated and was pulled over to the side. The hood was up, but no one was around the truck. Jeff pulled up behind them just after they got there, so he took over. They thought maybe he was calling in help from town. They evidently had not got back quite soon enough. I still managed to find some excitement on my own.

We loaded the semi-alive one in the back of Jim's pickup without moving the knife as it looked like it might cause more damage with us pulling it out than leaving it in place and loaded his dead buddy in beside him. We had placed a quilt in under the live one and hoped it kept him from rolling back and forth on the curves. Just because of Cary getting away, they restrained this one, just in case. None of us thought he could actually get up and jump over the side of a moving pickup, but maybe he could.

Teri stayed with me, just to make sure there were no more men hiding around the place, looking for whatever. We figured between what we had found before, in the outhouse and now this gun, we probably had already found what was being searched for.

After Jim left, I picked up my souvenirs and we headed back to the house. Teri looked at me carrying those two belts and I just shrugged and said I liked them.

I wonder how those guys got here and where is their transportation. Maybe someone had stayed in it and came over, saw all of us and grabbed Cary? Teri said they didn't see any vehicle along the road on their way back here. Maybe it is parked beyond my driveway.

Chapter 12

I put my trophies in the house and we take my pickup and drive north on the main road. We find signs of a struggle near a small turnout just past my drive. The grass and weeds are all tromped down and since the highway department never mows along here until just before snow hits in early winter, the tall weeds show where someone tussled around quite a bit. When we stop to look, there is quit a bit of blood all over the ground. Teri puts some of the bloody dirt in sample bags and numbers them after taking more pictures of the area.

There are tire tracks where someone really stomped on it to get away from this area. After she takes a lot of pictures, we widen our search around the area and find someone dumped over the bank. Dang, looks like Jim left too early. He could have put this one on the other side of his live passenger to hold him in place.

We ease down the bank to the body and it is alive yet. Neither one of us recognize him. Do we want to drag him back up the bank to the road or do we want to do like the first aid manuals advise and not move him and let him lay here until the professionals arrive in a few hours? We pull him up the bank where we can lay him out and check for wounds or bleeding. This far out of town, if someone is injured, they can die before the professionals arrive and the chances of living increase if someone will at least try to stop the bleeding or keep them warm.

Teri has some training and I have my first aid card, so we do know the bare bones basics. After checking him over, unless he has internal injuries we can't find, he should actually survive.

The amount of blood around the area is larger than his injuries indicate. So whoever took off in the vehicle may be bleeding quit a bit, also. We figure since we moved him this much, what the heck, we load him into the back seat of my pickup. We strap him down after Teri puts restraints on his wrists and legs. Then we head out in the direction the other vehicle went.

Less than a mile up the road, we find a vehicle off the side of the road. The driver is slumped over the steering wheel and looks totally out. He is lucky it is not one of the steep banks where he could have gone over and no one ever noticed.

We approach the SUV carefully and Teri has her gun drawn, just in case. When we get to the door, she holds the gun on the driver and I carefully reach in under and open the door. Cary falls out, unconscious. His head smacks the ground fairly firmly. If he wasn't out before, he would be now.

This guy must have at least nine lives. We

straighten him out a bit and check him over. He has been loosing blood from his original wounds that he was in the hospital for and evidently these tender fellows that he has been traveling with reopened to get him to talk. He looks like a few of his fingers may be broken, also. Some of the nails look raw and pulled. He might not be the most upstanding citizen, but no one should be treated like this if it is just over money. There may be quite a few other things I might be inclined to agree with these tactics over, but money isn't one of them. I probably should keep that opinion to myself.

We go ahead and bundle him into the back seat beside the other one. Teri restrains his wrists and legs, also. The people at the hospital are so going to yell at us for the treatment of these future patients. They are at least alive when we start out.

Amazingly enough, they are both still alive when we reach the hospital. The hospital staff have just finished working up the ones Jim and Grant brought in and here we are, with two more. Of course, one of his was dead already before the trip started. They are just pulling out of the parking lot as we arrive, so he circles around and parks to help us out here. They are amazed at our load. Cary looks a lot the worse for wear since the last time they saw him, even.

The police are going to have to manage a better system of security for these guys. The hospital had just turned in the report of Cary being missing from his room a little bit after Jim and Grant first got here. This time, when they put Cary in a bed, they fasten him to it. If someone takes him, they will have to take bed and all. I suppose that could be arranged if they are desperate enough. To my way of thinking, this may make it so they just kill him to keep him quiet if they can't take him out of here. I mention this and both Teri and Jim look surprised as though the thought had never entered their heads. Grant just nods yes. They check on Sheila, and she seems to be showing signs of finally coming around from her coma.

We finally get to leave the hospital. The staff are not sure whether they ever want to see us again or not. At least so far, none of us have been the ones requiring repairs and maintenance. This I am thankful for.

Since I have wasted the gas to come to town, I might as well buy some supplies and maybe I won't have to come in again for a month or two. Grant comes over to ride back out with me.

I make a few stops for assorted supplies for projects I am wanting to get done this summer and then for some groceries.

I am careful and check prices on each item I put in my cart. Grant grabs a cart and is busy adding stuff as we go up and down the aisles. I have a pretty good supply by the time I go to check out, but he has a mountain of food in his cart. He must really have a bad case of munchies. He tosses a cool chest on top his load and we head for checkout. He even pays cash for all of it. I pay cash, but I don't have a credit card and until I know for sure that all my clients payments are going to clear, I don't use checks.

We really have a load for my old pickup. The back seat is full as it can get and the bed has a pretty good load in it, also. I tarp and net the whole load.

We make it home without incident and I breath a sigh of relief. Nothing appears to be trashed, ruined or damaged while we were all gone. Maybe most of the ones responsible are finally dead or hospitalized. Of course I don't know if the ones we just hauled in are the ones responsible for listening in from their camp above the road. Grant told me on our way out that they found a regular listening post set up, when they went up the hill. Those guy didn't have time to go completely to town and get the SUV we recovered Cary out of, after their pickup overheated. There were only two men that came down the hill and left in the pickup, so maybe the third man was driving out after snatching Cary, picked them up and came back with them. We may never know. Somehow none of those guys look like the type to just volunteer information like that.

Grant told me when Cary came around some, he had a story similar to that. He really didn't now how they got him out of the hospital, but only one man had driven him out the road. They met the two men walking not long after they had left their pickup beside the road. He was coming around fairly well by then and remembered stopping to pick them up, then seeing their pickup along the road.

One of them noticed that Cary was awake and they pulled of and started asking him questions he couldn't answer, so they made sure to hit around his wounds to reopen them, then pulled a few fingernails and broke a couple of fingers. He was in and out of consciousness a bit and then they dragged him along with them to go check out the cabins, one more time.

He figured he was not long for this world and determined not to tell them what they wanted to know. He thought maybe they messed something up inside him as he didn't feel right inside. He wasn't sure exactly who was behind all of this, but he had suspicions. He did suggest they dig very deeply into John McCready's background and associates. Just before he passed out, he asked about Sheila and was upset that she was still unconscious. He should have thought of that before using her as a shield.

I don't say anything to Teri, when she gets back, about what Grant has told me. I don't want to get him in trouble for sharing, since I am not a cop.

I put everything away, after we unload my pickup. Then I go weed in my garden and greenhouse. No matter what, we have to eat. Having the fresh vegetables is well worth the effort. I would still like to get some chickens, a dog and a couple of cats. I can't figure out how to take care of them in my line of work, while I am out at hunt camp.

The guys are still fixing up the cabin Grant plans on staying in this winter. By the time they get done with it, it is going to be so nice I will be able to double the rent on it after he is gone.

I want a nice chef's salad for dinner, so bring in enough fresh greens and assorted other veggies to make it a really good one. I picked up some deli meats and cheeses so will boil a few eggs and fix a nice large platter of salad. I fix a large loaf of bread into garlic toast and have some leftover blueberry pie on hand for dessert.

I have the toast on the griddle as Teri, Jim and Grant come in. The table is set and the huge salad is in the center. It has enough meat, cheese and eggs on top to practically cover the lettuce, tomatoes, celery, scallions and broccoli florets. I suppose I should have asked if everyone likes salad, but hey, my sign should fix that problem and maybe someone else will be doing the cooking after this meal.

Darn, everyone liked it. Oh well, I actually enjoy cooking, so I don't really mind. The guys pick a good night to do the dishes, there aren't many. After dinner, I go back out and work in my greenhouse a while. My work around here has been neglected a lot this summer. Soon I hear the others out in the main garden, weeding. Instead of feeling sorry for not getting the things done I had planned, I should be thankful for all the help getting unplanned things done. My cabins have never looked better. One is now suitable for year around use. I would never have gotten all of that done and another building to be used as woodshed this winter, but will make a fine picnic area in the future.

I go on out and help weed on my garden. While we work, we talk and it gets around to why are all these goons showing up out here and what are they looking for? Who is financing them? Is it only one group or are there two, since they seem to be working independently of each other sometimes?

We toss around a lot of theories, but no one has any answers or would recognize them if they jumped out at us from one of our guesses. We can probably rule out locals, since no one recognizes any of the people we have caught or killed. I will probably have to go to Court on my shooting people. Everyone is pretty sure I won't have any problems, since it was pretty much them or me. I prefer saving me.

By the time we quit for the evening, the garden looks good and we are all going to have sore muscles tomorrow.

The next day is actually quiet. I am not used to this any more. It feels quite nice to just work around my place and not have anyone trying to trash a cabin or shoot at any of us. Teri says many days like this and they will have to go back to town, although Grant will probably stay.

A neighbor from a few miles up the road stops by with some chickens he wants to give me. He tells me they have made pets of them and can not stand to kill and eat them. His kids would cry and his wife would be upset at him if he even suggested it. So what I do with them is up to me, but he doesn't want to know about it. He has a couple of bags of feed and the large crate he brought them over in. If I will take them, he will even bring over their coop and the fencing he used in summer to let them out and be in the yard.

I tell him sure, I will take them. We unload the crate and he says he will be right back. A couple of hours later, he is back pulling a trailer with a very nice small building on it. It looks like a little cabin, and is well insulated even. We place it against one side of my house, so maybe I can figure out a way to get heat from my heater into the coop in winter. As he is putting the chickens from the crate into the coop, he is petting and talking to them and I am thinking he would be as upset if they are killed as his family would be.

The chickens snuggle in against him and make little noises in return and I can see they are very tame and gentle. Well, I have been wanting to get some chickens and now I have some. These are complete with feeders and watering containers, even. I ask him how much feed they need per month and grit and all the other stuff chickens need. He has a list already made out.

I must be the neighborhood soft touch when it comes to getting rid of pets. A couple of days later, another distant neighbor stops by and asks if I would like to have a dog. He has a sled dog that is a good dog, but not good enough for his team. He has the dog with him and the dog is very friendly. However, when Grant walks over from the cabins, the dog tenses up an growls low in his throat. I pet him, tell him he is a good dog and he is okay and he sits on my foot, between him and me, until after he observes him talking to us a while. The neighbor says he is a bit protective, also housebroke. I ask what his name is and he says Anuktuvik. He whirls around toward him, so he recognizes his name, but stays on my foot. I guess I have a dog.

Grant must figure my household isn't complete, because he shows up a week or so later, with a kitten. This has to be the cutest kitten ever born. Anuktuvik thinks it is just for him to care for and he washes it's face, much to it's disgust. Grant says he just could not resist it when he saw it. One of the clerks at the police station had a box full of them to give away. He thinks it is a female, but not sure.

She is silvery grey and has an almost flat face, but not a Persian. Her face looks almost like she chased a parked car. Her ears are slightly folded, but not as much as a scottish fold cat. She is quite a mixture but seems to have the cutest traits of each breed. She falls asleep between Anuktuvik's front feet and the dog stays still until the kitten wakes up.

Teri and Jim have been taken off duty out here and are back at work in town. Jeff stops by on his rounds, either direction, checking to see how things are going here. There have been no more incidents since that last dilly. Personally, I have had enough excitement to last me the rest of my life. Charging bears are not as scary. Usually they are not really charging, they are trying to get away from pain or doing a mock charge just to scare, which works. They scare me.

Grant has some project he is working on, but he does help out around here. He has been cutting and hauling more firewood for me and some more to supplement what he bought for himself for the winter. He says he enjoys weeding in the garden and is learning what is supposed to be left in there. He even checks out weeding in the greenhouse and watering.

We haul water from my little spring for the garden and he sets about digging a ditch to bring water over at least closer. He takes the next day off and goes to town. I figure he needs a bit of rest.

When he comes back, I am shocked. The man has rented a small track hoe. It is very small, but it certainly will be easier and faster than a shovel and grub hoe. He starts digging and soon has a nice little ditch and a pond if it holds water, near the edge of my garden. Then he digs a deep hole as far down as the hoe will reach, behind my house. He digs another, a bit farther away from my current cabins but where I want to construct others, in the future. He says we can build the outhouse first, there. He digs a hole beside the cabin he is living in, like the hole he dug by my house.

He proceeds to build and install wooden storage tanks, for greywater waste from our houses,, then covers then leaving a vent pipe sticking out. He thinks they should last 20 or 30 years.

That should help out a lot on the dishwater and

shower. Presently, I have an outdoor shower in the summer and a very basic winter shower using a 5 gallon bucket hung on a nail with a shower hose out the bottom and a large tub I stand in. Then I have to haul the water outside to dump after I am done. Sometimes in really cold weather, it is not worth the effort. Minus 40 degrees and still slightly damp from a shower is a good deterrent for going outside.

I ride back to town with him, when he returns the track hoe. We stop at the building supply store and I buy some more nails. 2x4s are on sale, so I add a unit of them. Then I find the shower stalls and put 2 of them on the order. We are set.

When we get back home, we unload the pickup and cover the stack of 2x4s. One of the showers is for my house and one for the cabin Grant is using. I have a small bathroom partitioned off in my place. He needs an area prepared to put his shower in his cabin. We finally decide to put it beside the kitchen counter, so the sink water and the shower water both can run into the buried tank.

We build the wall with can storage on the kitchen side. New cans go in the top and the oldest come out the bottom so they are always rotated in the correct order and easy to see when one is running low. His living room area will be smaller by the size of his mini-bathroom, but probably worth it.

Jim and Teri stop by on patrol and admire the new bathrooms. There are still only honey bucket set ups but the showers will be appreciated.

We visit a little while and I tell them no

unexplained happenings or unwanted visitors have occurred recently. Teri says Sheila is still out but is restless and eyes fluttering under her lids, so may be awake soon. Cary is actually in worse shape than Sheila. Emergency surgery was performed after we brought him in. When he was being worked over, his spleen was damaged and had to be removed. All the assorted goons are recovering that were delivered alive. Fingerprints identified most and they are all from out of state. Most are from Las Vegas.

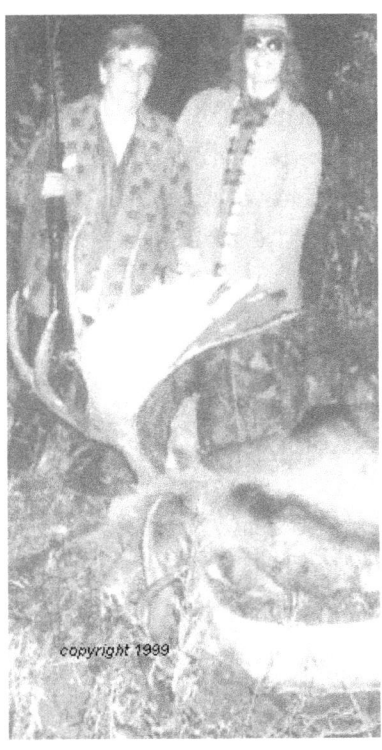

Chapter 13

After they leave, I go check my new little pond. I decide to add a gravel bank around it, so load up a bunch of buckets in my pickup and a shovel and head for the closest river bank. I haul 4 loads and am worn out. But I have the beginnings of a nice gravel bank around my little pond. I probably only need 50 or 60 more loads.

I wake up to sore muscles, but get right back to hauling river gravel. I add some large rocks to the load and place them around the back here and there, it is almost looking like the pond has been there forever.

In a slough along the road, I spot some cattails growing, so pull over and wade in to see about getting some to start growing around the edges of my pond. After finding the slough is a lot deeper than I thought and almost losing a shoe, I manage to get several tubers and pour a bucket of gravel into the bed of the truck to make sure the tubers don't dry out on their way to their new home.

I am still a wet muddy mess when I pull into my driveway and Grant is just coming out the door of his cabin. He waves me over so I stop. He looks at me in amazement. I must look even worse than I thought. He reaches over and pulls some duckweed out of my hair.

He gets in my pickup and I drive on over to unload. Since I am already wet and muddy, I wade right into the pond to plant my cattails. I toss the duckweed into the pond, also. Grant starts unloading the buckets of gravel.

We spread the gravel around the edges of the pond and it is looking pretty good. Maybe I can find more plants that are edible and like moist growing conditions. I'm hoping the cattails make it.

We go in the house and I start fixing some lunch. The dog and the kitten are asleep together under the front window in a patch of sunshine. The chickens have been laying eggs, so I have nice fresh eggs and make egg salad sandwiches for lunch.

After lunch, I start on improving the chicken run and making their coop better for winter. I have an old cat battery that looks rough but still holds a full charge, so set it up on my sun porch. I have a small solar panel set and place it in the south facing windows and hook up the battery to them to keep it fully charged. I will use it for some light in the coop to help the chickens through the winter. I will get a couple of buckets of finer gravel on my next trip to the river and keep it handy for the chickens, also.

I start cutting grass seed heads to dry for the chickens for winter. I will get them regular feed also, but figure this will supplement their feed and maybe be good for them. I wouldn't want to harvest large quantities the way I am doing this, but it works okay for the small amount I am planning on getting.

I start getting things ready for my fall hunts. Now that I have animals, I am worried about what to do with them. Grant volunteers. Since the case is still open and he is technically supposed to be watching for any more "visitors" looking for whatever it was they were looking for, he will stay here and also feed the animals. That takes care of that problem.

Until he says he is staying and I relax all over, I didn't realize how tense I have been. Worry about coming home to a pile of ashes or everything just trashed has been at the back of my mind since all of this started.

My moose hunts are usually a bit farther north. I haul my 4 wheeler ATVs up on a trailer when I go set up the camp. We don't hunt from the ATVs, but they do assist getting into the areas where we start walking and also come in handy for retrieving the game we harvest. The bigger the moose, the farther from the road, when he is harvested.

Grant is a walking set of questions while I am packing the pickup and trailer. He wants to know the how and why of every item I pack. I feel like I am giving a basic course in Arctic survival and hunting. He is so interested that it doesn't even bother me. I don't even flip him when he touches my arm. There went rules number 1 and 2.

While he asks questions, he is helping me pack. The job goes much faster with the 2 of us working, so we break early for lunch. All through lunch he asks more questions about hunting and hunt camps. He will know how, long before he actually gets out there to do any of it. He is a hunter, but he has always hunted open spaces and desert country. Nothing like muskeg to thin out the wimps and wussies.

That's probably why I try to keep my hunts up in the higher country away from the rivers and low lying areas. I would like my clients to want to come back and to pass along good words to their buddies that may be looking for a hunting guide.

Somehow, he starts talking about politics, even though I always try to keep from discussing or cussing about political issues. I tell him we have enough public serpents in office. He laughs and I change the subject.

He rides along to see where my hunt camp will be and to see more of the country. He asks why I chose this spot and why am I setting up camp in this particular area. He could write a book by the time we are done setting up. I finally ask him why the interrogation?

He actually sort of blushes. "I'm sorry, I just am fascinated by the whole thing and never expected to actually get to be in on how it is done and get to talk to a person that really does know how to do all of this stuff. Alaska has always been my dream and to be here doing all of this is just mind boggling."

"Okay, I get that, but can we enjoy a few moments of silence once in a while?" Now I've hurt his poor little feelings, oh geez.

Chapter 14

I go to the airport to pick up my first clients and find they have brought another person with them. He tries to be buddy, buddy with them and they act scared of him.

When we stop to pick up their licenses after I get the balance of my fee, it clears and they all sign my waivers, I pull up at the State Troopers Headquarters. I take my keys when I go in, leaving them in my pickup. I am surprised to see all three are still in the truck when I get back. Jeff is off-duty and ready to go hunting as my assistant. I've given him my ideas about our extra "guest".

Jeff was going to bring his own Jeep, but now he decides to ride with me. Neither of us wants to stop at my home with this guy.

When we pull in to hunt camp, the guy seems surprised. Does he think we hunt from my home? The other two men are getting more relaxed now that we are in camp. One of them wanted to hunt grizzlies, but when I sold him the hunt, I only agreed to hunt for moose, if a nice grizzly came around and he bought the tags, he could get it. While we are putting our gear away, he gets that chance.

A large blond male is wandering pretty close to camp. I get the client and we go observe the bear as it makes it's way closer. Suddenly the bear turns and disappears into the brush and I turn in time to see the extra client waving out his sleeping bag.

When I walk up to him, I am steamed and he just stands there smirking and I want to cause some damage but I don't.

I smile at him which seems to upset him, then I turn and go into my tent. Later, Jeff asks me to never smile like that at him, just shoot him instead. He figured that bear had a better nature right now.

I prepare our evening meal and we eat in near silence. My actual client is upset about not getting the grizzly, the other one feels bad for him and the actual jerk that caused the miss is still smirking. His excuse was that he wanted to air out his sleeping bag and didn't think the instructions to keep quiet and hold still referred to him also.

We are all sitting around a nice fire later that evening, the jerk on one side with his back towards the brush and all of us on the other side with camp behind us. I spot some movement in the brush behind the jerk. I whisper to my clients and Jeff to hold still and for the client to slowly raise his rifle to where he can use it if necessary. Somehow I manage not to warn the jerk on the other side of the fire.

The bushes part and the bear sticks his head out right behind the jerk. Even I am surprised, it is a different bear.

As the bear rears up on his hind legs, my client is raising his rifle and the jerk's eyes go huge and round. He is positive he is about to be shot. The bear woofs behind him, he whirls around and the bear drops back into the brush.

My client, slowly lowers his rifle and the jerk is goggle eyed and sweating. We spend the rest of the evening telling bear stories. The kind on a par with ghost stories at a kids camp. There won't be much sleeping soundly tonight.

Next morning is opening day for moose and we get up very early to go out. Jeff gets the jerk and I take the other two out. Jeff says they will mainly tromp through the brush and won't see anything at all.

My clients and I hike up on a high ridge to glass the valleys on both sides. These two drew straws the night before to see who had first try at a bull. This one really wants a moose and the other one mainly still wants a grizzly. Since the grizzlies seem to be thicker than the moose, he may have a good chance at one, yet.

We see two very nice bulls feeding down in the valley opposite our camp and decide to try for them early tomorrow.

We hike back to camp and I start the evening meal. Jeff and the jerk hike in just as dinner is done. The jerk looks totally worn out and is puffing hard. His face is all red and he is sweating like he just ran a couple of miles. Jeff looks like he has just been out for a stroll.

He is smiling as they walk into camp. The way the jerk is puffing, I figure we will have a heart attack happening around here fairly soon. He plops down on a log near the fire and promptly falls asleep. Or maybe it's a coma, nah, just wishful thinking.

I let him sleep 15 minutes, then wake him up to eat and point him to his tent. He eats like he has not seen food in weeks and then immediately crawls into his tent and we soon hear him snoring. The Guide I used to work for claimed snoring drew bears. If so, we have a prime caller going on right here.

My two and I are out hiking after an early breakfast just before daylight gets fully bright. It is light enough to shoot if we see a legal moose, but we should be in the area we want to be, before the moose bed down for the day.

Since there were two large legal sized bulls together, both clients are prepared. When we break over the hill near the area we saw them yesterday, there they are. They are feeding in our direction, so we sit down in a handy spot with good cover and watch them approach. The best part of this is, they are feeding toward camp. Each step taken will be one step we won't have to pack them later.

We wait until they start to turn up a small side valley, then both my clients score. Now the real work begins.

We take a lot of pictures and both men had taken video earlier and I used one of their cameras while they set up and shot. So they will have plenty to share with their families. Once the filming is over, we start on the work of butchering. There will be plenty of good food for a whole year at least from all this meat and the bulls were not in rut yet, so it will be excellent eating.

I suggest one of the men head back to camp and see if Jeff is there to come help us. They tell me to go ahead, they are enjoying their whole adventure. I explain how to proceed and where to cut and they get right on it.

I hike into camp and the jerk is looking very rough. I ask Jeff if he wants to come assist us. I offer the jerk the chance to be there, also, he just moans.

Jeff said he offered to take him out this morning and thought the guy was going to shoot him for asking. Seems he isn't in very good shape. I'm not sure we should leave him in camp alone, but I would like to get back to my hunters and get this meat all packed to camp. We will hang it back in the trees as high as we can, to deter bears.

When I get back to camp with my pack of meat, the jerk is just coming out of my tent. I yell at him and ask what he thinks he is doing. He looks so miserable when he says he is looking for painkillers, aspirin, anything, that I actually believe him. I tell him there is some OTC meds in the cook tent by the water cooler and he can get some from there. He nods and heads for the cook tent.

I go on through camp and start up the ladder to hang the meat. I hear crashing in the underbrush off to my left, so throw my hook over the bar above me and get the load off my back and my gun out. I still the swaying of the meat so no motion will give away my position. The crashing sounds are coming closer and I finally make out a large black bear being chased by a very large grizzly. Their ranges overlap here and grizzlies will make a meal of the blacks if given a chance. It tends to give the black bears some attitude and they can be very dangerous.

The bears have barely cleared the edge of camp when my client with the grizzly tag steps into view. He never hesitates, after he sees me give a thumbs up. He pulls up his rifle and shoots his grizzly.

He is a very good shot and the bear is down. I keep watch on the area he fell in and the man brings his load of meat on over to hang. We get the load up beside mine and then we carefully approach the fallen grizzly. We walk up from his back and I carefully reach over and poke him with my rifle barrel. The client has his rifle at the ready and we slowly go around to poke the bear's eye with the rifle. If he has any life in him, he will respond to that.

No one wants a bear to suddenly wake up halfway through skinning it. Could really mess up a day for all involved.

We get some photos while the bear is still able to be moved around and then position him so we can skin him after we finish the moose. This is going to be a very long day.

I quickly start a moose roast going on one of my

trips packing meat and add a bunch of potatoes, onions and carrots. The dutch oven goes in the fire pit beside the main fire and should be ready in a few hours. We eat our lunches on the walk back to get more meat, since we already had the sandwiches with us for the day when we started out this morning.

By evening, we are all just about beat and we still have the grizzly to skin. I get started making the initial cuts to make sure he gets the best shaped rug possible. Jeff comes over to spell me after a while so I can complete getting dinner. I'm really glad we still have fairly long days and the light holds well into the evenings.

The next morning, the jerk still doesn't want to go out hunting. I ask him what he wants to do the rest of his hunt time. He growls he would really rather just go back to town. After looking at the size of a moose and the rack, he don't think he has any place to display it if he did get one. I ask about his expense that he has into the hunt and he says it don't even matter, he wants to go to town. Well, okay then.

The other two don't want to just sit around camp and would rather be in town also. It doesn't matter to me, just a few more days I don't have to feed them and they do have what they came here for. We start packing the pickup and loading the meat. The men tell me they really don't want the meat, they have no way to transport it all home. I will keep a half of one and donate the rest to the food bank in town. I don't have electricity or a freezer but in the next few days before the next client comes in, I will can and dehydrate a lot of what I want to keep. I'll make a lot of jerky, also.

We make good time on our way to town and stop by Fish & Game to have the grizzly hide and skull sealed so the client can take it out of state or have it tanned here. I give him my taxidermy brochure and he looks relieved and immediately gives me a deposit for making him a rug. We head directly over to the tannery and leave the hide there to be tanned. He even prepays for that. Wish there were more clients like that.

The jerk wanted dropped off at a hotel as soon as we hit town, so he was not with us at the tannery or F&G so I ask my client how he happened to get saddled with bringing him along as they didn't exactly act like friends. He stammered a bit and said he had gambling debt and they agreed to forget about it if he let this guy come along on his hunt.

I drop these two at a different hotel and go to the food bank. They are happy to see some fresh meat and in good condition. I tell them I want to keep half of one moose and we pick out which pieces I will keep and they take the rest inside to take care of.

I finally get home with the meat and start packing the pieces inside right away. Grant comes over to help and we soon have the meat piled on counters and some on the table, also.

My pets are happy to see me and I have to share my bed with them tonight. They don't want to be any farther from me than necessary. I've missed them also and the kitten has grown, I'm sure.

I stick a large chunk in a pan ad put it in the oven to roast for the flavor. Then I start boning out several of the larger bones and sawing them in half. Then they get added to the meat in the oven to make sure the bones will add roasted flavor to the stock I will make and can later.

I set up my grinder on the table and soon there is a mound of ground meat ready to be browned. I get that on and add dried onions, celery and green peppers. After the burger has browned, I add a couple of #10 cans of diced tomatoes and some tomato sauce and it is ready to can. It doesn't take long to have meat ready for the whole next year, doing it this way.

Grant helps out very well and is great on the grinder. As soon as I show him how I want the meat sliced for jerky, he gets right on that. I mix up some marinade and the slices go directly into the marinade. In the morning, they will go into the smokehouse. I have 3 days before my next clients come in. This meat has to be done by then.

The canners are kept going the next 3 days. I have made Spanish sauce, using small finger sized pieces of steak in a tomato based sauce with black olives and mushrooms. I also made some stroganoff that will only require heating and adding sour cream to serve over noodles. We grind more into burger and I make pizza sauce with added pepperoni slices in part of it and sliced hot links in the other half.

The hamburger patties take the most time to make. They have to be made to slide into a wide mouth jar, but have to be cooked first. The moose burger is very lean, so they don't shrink much while baking. All the roast has been sliced and canned in the pan juices. The bones are put on to boil with the roasted bones and some seasonings.

Grant is having a time and learning to can quite well. The jerky is ready to sample before we are done with all the canning.

By the time I have to go pick up the next week's clients, all that is left to can is the broth and whatever meat scraps are stuck to the bones and falls off into the broth while cooking. It is concentrated down and will make excellent soups and stews this coming winter.

Jeff has brought his Jeep out here from town, so he will have it here, after this next hunt or even can take it to camp which could be handy. He tells us that the jerk was drinking in the hotel bar when someone walked up behind him and shot him twice under the ear with a small caliber handgun. No one saw the shooter. I didn't like the guy, but that is a little extreme.

The drive to town is the first time I have been alone in over a week. I have really missed that. This whole summer has not been very relaxing. I am looking forward to winter so much.

The clients plane is late, landing. So I have time to get something to eat. I do a bit of grocery shopping also, so I have cut it a bit fine returning to the airport. Their plane is landing as I park my truck.

Chapter 15

These two men seem very nice and we get the waivers signed, the licenses and tags purchased and are on our way out of town in good time. One fellow is quite elderly but in fairly good condition and the other man is middle aged but looks like he has worked hard all his life.

We stop at my place and they are charmed by the little rental cabins and my whole place. They ask if we can spend the night here and continue to camp in the morning. I guess we can, since they are the clients and they are paying for the trip.

They get settled into the cabin that everyone has been searching. It is certainly clean now. I go home and start dinner for everyone.

I kept out a good portion of moose meat that I tenderized and make into chicken fried steaks and make cream gravy on the pan drippings. My garden is still producing so I make a nice large green salad to have with the mashed potatoes.

After dinner, I dig up part of the row of leaf lettuce and transplant into a window box in the house. We will be getting a killing frost any night now and I really enjoy having my salads and lettuce for my sandwiches as late into the winter as possible.

We get a very early start for hunt camp. As we are pulling in to camp, we see a bull moose walking through the trees on the other side of the small valley. I am never able to see him clearly enough to make sure he is legal or not.

The younger client and I take our rifles and my backpack and head out to see while Jeff finishes unloading the pickup and his Jeep and makes the older client comfortable.

My client and I circle around and get a good look at the bull. He is not a legal bull for out of state hunters. He would be fine for a resident hunter though. Jeff and I are not allowed to hunt while we have clients in the field which pretty much makes sure we never get our own meat for the winter. I am always happy when client lets me keep some or all of the meat.

While we are out here, we climb up the hill far enough to glass over the entire valley. I have a spotting scope in my pack and set it up so we can take turns checking out all the area. We see some cows over near the bluffs to the right. That is an area we should check tomorrow. It may have more bulls starting to hang around.

While we are sitting here, relaxing, we hear a shot from the area near camp. We look at each other and then hear another shot from the same area. We start back down the hill toward camp.

We hear two more shots as we get closer to camp. Somehow, neither of us thinks these are from hunters or even from our hunters, but we need to check it out.

When we reach a small hill near camp, we climb up it carefully and lay down to peek over the top into camp. It appears that someone is intent on taking out Jeff and the elderly client. Jeff and Joe are down behind a dirt hummock, unable to go right or left while two men over near the road are circling around for a better view of the camp and their victims. My client, Jerry, and I each pick a target and open fire. We cause some damage as both men disappear from sight and there was a scream that sounded really terrible. Jerry and I look at each other and start on down the hill.

Jeff is helping Joe get seated in a chair and asks Jerry to stay with him while Jeff and I go check out what is out in the woods.

We find where both men had been and there is quite a bit of blood in both areas where they fell so both are injured. We continue tracking and find them near a car parked in the edge of the road. They are not dead, but not in good condition either. We search for weapons, check their wounds and stop most of the bleeding. After loading them into the backseat of the car, Jeff restrains them, just in case they get irritable about the situation and takes them to town.

I go back to camp and check Joe to make sure he really is okay. He seems to be fine, just surprised to get shot at in the wilderness of Alaska. It is not a place a person expects random shootings. So maybe it isn't random.

I think I am going to have to advertise in different areas, my clientele seems to be just a little bit shady to put it nicely.

Jeff returns in a few hours. Jim and Teri have given him a ride out. Teri takes a long range photo of my clients to run through their computer program and see who they really are. Oh great. I finally get two that seem nice and they are probably on the Ten Most Wanted list.

Jeff and I walk back to camp and he says both the men lived to get admitted to the hospital. Neither one was in good shape though. Both were small scale hoods from the Lower 48.

While he was there, he checked on Cary and Sheila. Neither one is doing very well. Seems every time they show signs of improvement, something happens to set them back again. The hospital is really beefing up security and now it is more like entering a high security facility just to go visit someone or check in.

We are up and starting out on the day's hunt just at daylight. Jeff and Joe hike up on the small knoll Jerry and I shot the men from yesterday. It gives a fair view of the immediate valley and they just might spot a nice bull from there. Jerry and I hike toward the area we glassed the cows in, yesterday.

We reach a good place to glass the area from and set up the spotting scope. As we concentrate on the area we are glassing, it is almost like yesterday allover again, there is a shot from near camp.

We look at each other and grab the spotting scope and head back toward camp. This time the shot meant that Joe had his moose. A beautiful 60 inch rack at least. We spend the rest of the day skinning and butchering out his trophy. I cut off some small steaks and start them marinating in camp on one of our trips by to hang the meat. The next trip, I wash and wrap some potatoes in foil. The next trip, I place the potatoes in the coals of the fire.

By the time we are done packing, the potatoes are about done and I thread the steaks on peeled green sticks and hand each person their own to broil over the coals of the fire. The men enjoy dinner very much and we are all more than ready to get some sleep by the time we are done eating.

The next morning, Jerry and I finally make it over where the cows were the last two days. We don't see any cows, but we soon hear a bull thrashing the brush near us. Soon after, another one starts across the little valley from us. We find a little higher ground and set up the scope again. Both bulls are fairly large. Maybe not quite as large as the one Joe got yesterday, but Jerry is happy with the size. He picks the one closest to us and we start our stalk. I think we could probably have just walked right up to them both. They were so intent on each other they paid no attention to us.

Stalking them seemed more professional, so we stalked them and Jerry made a nice clean shot. We walk down and take several nice pictures and then start working. I bag up the first pieces of meat cut off and send Jerry back to camp to have Jeff bring a 4 wheeler out since we finally got one in an area they could reach.

I continue skinning and have the bull mostly skinned and both legs and backstrap removed on that side. I cut the head loose and turn the moose over onto the other side, and continue skinning. Sounds like an odd way to do it, but it works very well and one person can handle a moose without being a mess by the time they are done.

By the time they get back with the 4 wheelers, we can start loading and hauling while the skinning continues. The battery powered sawzall was on the 4 wheeler basket so I cut the ribs into short ribs while still attached, and we bag them up with the heart and liver.

When we leave the site, there isn't much left but it will be a feast for the ravens and jays. If any bears are still hanging around, they will be drawn to the remains, also. I just hope they stay away from camp. The antlers go in on the last load. Antlers have to remain in the field until all the meat is salvaged.

We are very tired that evening so no one stays up late after the evening meal. I hear a few sounds late in the night, but after not hearing anything else, I figure it is just small animals moving through the brush around the camp, looking for the source of the meat odors.

As I open my tent flap on my way out in the morning, a flash blinds me and a voice asking what it's like to harbor one of America's top crime bosses from a shape behind a mic shoved into my face, greets me. I get a grip on the hand holding the mic and drag it into my tent with a gasp from the other end of the arm. The mic gets ripped from her grasp and crushed underfoot and she is getting indignant. I turn toward her and tell her I could have just shot her. She turns white and I figure she is about 2 seconds from passing out, I push her down into a chair and ask her just what the heck she thinks she is doing?

She says she got an anonymous tip to be out here are daylight for the story of her career. I told her she may have just got lucky to not BE the story of her career as we have been having troubles and several people have already been shot.

From the sounds outside my tent, Jeff is taking care of the photographer. Then he says "Knock, knock." I tell him to enter and he pushed the photographer in ahead of him. My tent is getting very crowded. Jeff has deleted the picture taken of me off the photographers camera, so at least I won't have that particular one plastered all over the newspaper.

While Jeff keeps them in my tent, I walk over to the clients tents and from outside, ask if they are up. Both say yes and I ask them to come walk with me a little bit. They both step out carrying their weapons and we walk out past the camp quite a ways. I tell them we have been singled out for media attention and ask what they would like to do next? I don't mention America's crime boss or any of that stuff.

The two men step aside a bit and after talking things over in low tones, they ask if I would mind cutting the hunt short and hauling them both back to town, right now? I can do that. I have my personal stuff locked in my truck anyway, so we carefully walk back into camp, they pull their bags out and we hike on out to the truck. The younger man stops a minute by the car parked nearby and then joins us at the pickup. He says don't worry, it will just take them quite a while to get back to town now. Nothing permanent. I leave a short note on Jeff's Jeep visor and we head for town.

On the way to town, I complain just a little bit about how the summer has gone and wonder why I am being hassled so much. Joe looks at me and says I will not be hassled any more. He seems so positive that I believe him.

They ask to be taken straight to the airport and as soon as we are in cell phone range of town, Jerry is on the phone arranging travel. The moose antlers are still in camp, so I ask what they want done with them. They look perplexed and suggest I keep them and if they ever get to come back, they can pick them up from my place. Uh, okay.

When I pull up at the terminal, they jump out, grab their bags and hand me an envelope. I open the envelope after I stop at a grocery store and the amount of cash in it is mind boggling. There is a note also. They thank me for a very relaxing time and hope to be able to come back one day. If they are crime lords, at least they have good manners.

I am almost back to camp before I meet the reporter and photographer. They are not happy looking. When I reach camp, Jeff is over in the trees near the area we park in. He says he searched all around the camp and only found a few bugs. The multi-legged kind, not the listening type.

We start breaking down camp. Moose season is almost over and with the reporter showing up here, we will probably have more problems cropping up if we stay. I would rather take all this meat home and take care of it, anyway. I will share it with others that haven't been able to get any meat.

While we are loading the meat in my pickup, an older truck pulls up and a couple that live farther out the road ask if I need a hand. I accept, even though we are almost done and offer them a half if they can use it. They have not had any luck on their hunting and depend on it for most of their meat for the winter. I know they won't accept a whole moose, and not without at least helping some on loading mine. They accept and I make sure they get the largest pieces we have. I offer them the bag of ribs and organ meat. They are very happy and so am I. I would like to have given them more but tried that in the past.

An older couple live between hunt camp and home and we stop and drop off another quarter of the moose. They are cutting it up to can before we get back out to the main road.

One last stop on the way home at a family that are having some tough times. Another quarter stays there when we leave.

At home, we unload my reduced load of meat into my kitchen. The camping gear is stored in the shed behind the house.

I decide to grind most of it into burger and make more meat sauce, and more hamburger patties to can. The bones are started roasting in the oven, to make stock on for canning.

I saved out enough to make chicken fried steaks for dinner and have them breaded and ready by the time the first canner is ready to take off the stove. I start the next canner while cooking the steaks and fixing a salad. I still have some rolls from what I baked for camp, so I heat them up to have with dinner.

Jeff and Grant come over while I am preparing dinner, so stay and have some with me. We talk a bit about the last clients. Jeff has items with the men's fingerprints on them to check those out in town when he goes in. I suppose I should turn over the wad of cash they gave me as a hunt tip, but it is accepted practice to tip the Guide on a successful hunt.

Both clients were successful, but they gave me an extra large tip, anyway. I bring out the envelope, note and cash and show Jeff and Grant. They whistle at the amount and I tell them I have handled it, but if they need it for fingerprints, some others may still show up. Jeff thinks he has enough for that without my tip. I didn't realize I was holding my breath until he says keep it.

By the time I take off the last canner for this evening, I am completely tired out. I set the rest of the meat out on the porch to stay cool and the pets and I head for bed. There is a tap at the door and I really don't want company now. I grab a gun and go see who it is at this time of night. I don't see anyone. A flutter of paper catches my attention and I finally open the door a crack to see what it is. I look around to see if anyone is still in the area, even checking the rearview mirrors I have set up so I can see if a bear is near the house but out of my sight before coming outside. I finally get brave enough to reach out to grab it and pull it inside, slamming and locking the door as fast as I can. I never said I was brave.

Chapter 16

What the heck? It is the title to a new pickup, in my name, with a sticky note attached saying "sorry for the inconveniences this summer." I think I am already asleep and will wake up in the morning to find it has been a weird dream. I leave the papers on the table and go on to bed.

The papers are still there when I wake up and go out to start the coffee. I get the next canner of meat going and walk out to the cabins to see what Jeff and Grant have to say about it.

There is a beautiful midnight blue 4 wheel drive crew cab pickup sitting in the driveway. It even has extra fuel tanks added. I knock on Grants cabin door. He and Jeff are having breakfast. I show them the note and the title and point to the pickup out by the road. They hadn't noticed it earlier this morning.

When we walk out to it, the motor is still warm. Two sets of keys are on the floor mat in front of the drivers seat. The numbers match the title. While we are standing there looking at it, the brush rattles on the other side of the road and a man steps out. He isn't paying attention and is adjusting himself. He spots us and looks embarrassed. "Sorry, needed to use the bushes and didn't know anyone would be out here at this time of day. It's been a long drive and now I have to wait for someone from Fairbanks to come get me."

Jeff asks him where he drove from and he says Anchorage, to deliver this truck. The old man wanted it brought out as a surprise for his granddaughter, he said. He said the old man didn't look too healthy and his flight south was delayed by the volcano spewing south of Anchorage. The old man wanted to buy a nice present for the girl and wanted it delivered as soon as possible. He sent the title up by air as flights were still going north.

Jeff offers him a ride in with him as he has to go back in anyway with the evidence bags he has. The man accepts. Jeff takes the title in with him. I take a few pictures of the pickup as I may not get to actually keep it, I guess.

Then I remember my canner and run back to the house. It is rocking away but I have to start the time from now since I don't know when it actually started. Anuktuvik and Kivalina are happy to see me back already. Poor animals don't know what to expect from me after my being gone to hunt camp so much the last 2 weeks.

I put the roasted bones on to boil for soup stock and add onions, celery, garlic and some fresh herbs. The meat sauce is almost all canned now, so my pantry is looking much better for the winter.

After boiling a few hours, I set the stock aside to cool enough to chop the meat left on the bones after removing them, returning the meat to the pot and boil down a bit more to concentrate it better. By tomorrow, I should be done with the moose.

Jeff still has some time left on his vacation leave, so he comes back out. They called the dealer where the pickup was bought. It was paid for with a legitimate credit card by an elderly gentleman. Now that is some credit card.

He hands back the title and says congratulations, you have a new truck. Wow.

This elderly gentleman told the driver I was his granddaughter but as far as I know, my grandparents are all deceased, long ago. I think it might be Joe from the hunt. He was a nice seeming fellow and we got along well in camp. But the tip and now the truck seem a bit excessive. The tip I could chalk up to my getting him away from the reporter and to the airport with no hassles and a lot of speed. The truck I have almost no idea about. Maybe a faint niggling in the back of my mind.

Where did that reporter get her tip about my client and was he who she said he was? She told Jeff she got an anonymous tip to come check it out. She decided on her own to bring a photographer and do the whole shock interview thing. At least I didn't just shoot her.

We take the truck for a spin and it is a dream to drive. It even has heated seats. I should probably never have driven it, if they decide it should be impounded as evidence or something, I may cry.

After parking the truck, we go in and have some coffee. It has been a strange couple of days. For that matter, it has been a very strange summer. I really hope to never have another even remotely similar. I'm praying for a calm, boring winter.

I continue getting my place ready for winter. There aren't too many jobs left needing done, but I like having the garden all cleaned up and ready to plant next season. The greenhouse also needs cleaned and the beds renewed. The chicken coop gets a good cleaning and all the stuff cleaned out goes under the dirt in the greenhouse. The hard freezing is holding off a bit and I manage to get all these chores done without fighting frozen dirt and chicken droppings.

The buckets of gravel I have stashed along the side of the coop, well covered to keep them dry. That will give the chickens some grit throughout the winter for digestion. My next trip to town I will haul lots of feed and try for some straw for them, too.

I drain my storage water tanks outside and fill several buckets to keep in the house for wash-up water and cleaning.

The 4 wheelers are serviced, parked and covered for the winter. I turn the tents wrong side out and air them over the clothesline a few days to make sure they are well aired and dry before storing them for the winter. When I unroll the sleeping bags and toss them over the clothesline, a small bundle drops out on the ground. Now what?

I'm getting leery of just picking up anything, so I grab a plastic bag and slip my hand into it before using it to pick up the little bundle. I'm not even sure which sleeping bag it fell out of and who used that bag. I pull the plastic bag over it and take it in the house. After tying a knot in the plastic bag, I hang the bag and contents on one of the hooks behind my door and put the coats back over it until I figure out what to do, then promptly forget it.

I finish airing out all the camping gear and put it all away so it will be ready to use for the spring hunts.

I pay Jeff for his help in the field and put the information in my files for tax purposes, next year. I'm going to have to actually fix up a home office at this rate. The shoe box method won't work if I keep expanding.

Jeff has to be on duty the next morning, so he goes back to town. I've almost gotten used to having so many people around.

Grant is good about staying out of my way and in his cabin or out doing whatever he wants to be doing. I continue preparations for winter. I go cut a load of spruce poles to use for building, They work well for wall studs. I cut them to 12 foot lengths and stack them on pallets. When I limbed them, I pretty much peeled them, too. Not a pretty job, but it works. I will cover the pile after it freezes up and before snow.

Grant wants to get internet for the winter and the cabin is set to far back in the trees for him to get it. He asks if he pays to have it installed on my home, and then has a wireless box aimed at his cabin, can he go ahead and do it? That might be nice, I just have never been able to afford it. There is also the fact that I will have to run a generator for the hours he wants to be on line. He says he will supply the fuel if I will run my generator for 4 hours each evening.

I better get to town and haul out most of the feed I will need this winter for the chickens, kitten and dog. I would rather not have to go to town at all for most of the winter. Actually, I would rather never go to town.

I go in and while there, find a used laptop, cheap. If there is going to be internet in my home, I might as well see if I can put up a website for my hunts. I also buy enough feed for the entire winter., I hope.

A few days later, the satellite internet fellow shows up and puts a dish up on my roof, aimed almost due south southeast. That is one of the main things I notice when I go to the Lower 48, the dishes all point up, instead of aimed at the horizon.

Grant comes over and helps him install it and then the box for wireless. They show me how to use it with my laptop and I am in business.

Internet is a whole new experience for me, so I will be learning a lot here. Both men warn me about opening links and some mail or sites. Grant sets me up with an email account and then goes in and shows me how to find things. He offers to scan some of my hunt pictures but I actually do have a digital camera, so can now put them on it, too. When we are putting the pictures from the camera onto the laptop, we stop at some I took in camp while no one was noticing. I have some excellent ones of Jerry and Joe.

We enlarge them and these are better than any mug shots. Grant sends them to Jim, in town. While he is at it, he sends our new email addresses and now we are linked to the outside world. I am not sure I like this.

Teri and Jim stop by on their next shift along this road. They have some information for me. Seems maybe the old guy really is my grandfather. Also seems he might be involved a bit in the underworld in some way although they have no proof of that. He also paid the gift tax on the pickup he bought for me.

I thought I didn't have any family left and now this. It is a bit of a shock. From an orphan to someone that has some family, maybe a lot of family, is quite a surprise. I might do some searching for information on line tonight, might as well learn how it works.

I start with my Mom and Dad. I find their death certificates and go back from there. They led very private lives, so there isn't much available about them on-line. It does list their parents and my mother's father is listed as Joseph J. Parnetti, estranged from his daughter even before she met my father and they married.

The information on Joseph was varied and listed his occupation as investment consultant. He had been questioned over the years about some dealings, but nothing ever held up in Court.

The photographs in the articles were of my client, showing the aging process as I scanned through the records. He had not been hauled into Court for many years now. Either he was retired or better at staying in the background.

Mom was evidently his only child and she left soon after her mother died. There was no explanation for why she left or why she stayed away. When I was a child and asked about other family, she always said there wasn't any. I guess it is past time for me to go through the box of personal papers from my Mom that I brought home after her funeral.

Chapter 17

I shut down the internet and go dig through my closet to find the box. It is a fairly heavy box so I just drag it out to the kitchen table. I stack papers and file folders on the table from the box. Most, I have no idea what it even pertains to. I will have to go through each one page by page.

At the bottom of the box, I find an old 5 year diary, like teen girls used to keep before internet and cell phones. The diary sounds like a whole different world. She didn't remember her mother ever standing up for her self, the house was dominated by her father and house-hold help did all the work around the house. Her mother was a pale shadow in the background but she loved her.

After her mother died, her father expected her to step in as hostess but to keep her mouth shut and not have opinions. She started flirting with one of the guards and her father had him beat and dismissed. Since the guard had nothing to do with it, she was furious and had a screaming tirade with her father and was locked in her room.

She packed her bags, threw them out her window one night, crawled out the window and along the ledge to another section of roof that sloped down closer to the ground, eased herself over the edge and dangled a bit, afraid to let go, until her fingers refused to grasp any longer and she dropped the few feet left to the ground.

She hobbled over to her bags, jammed the scattered items from the one that popped open back into the bag and made her way down to the road below the house. A friend she went to school with picked her up and took her to her house for the night while they planned how she could disappear.

They cut her long hair very short and dyed it. Then they traded a lot of clothes. After her hair was dry, they snuck out of the house and her friend took her to a bus station and one was leaving in a few minutes. She didn't care where it was going, just as long as she was gone as soon as possible. The next stop, she changed buses and names and went a different direction until she finally ended up in Oregon.

By the time she met my dad, she was back to using her own name and working as a waitress at a small out of the way truck stop on the highway between Bend and Burns, Oregon. His parents owned a ranch nearby and he started hanging around. They would talk about traveling away from there and ended up deciding Alaska sounded like the best place for both of them.

The diary ended there.

Nothing sounded like my Mom. She was a sweet quiet woman and my Dad adored her. They worked together and ran an old roadhouse down along the main highway. They died in the fire that took the old historic site.

Chapter 18

I put the diary in the lock box in the back of my closet and leave all the files in another box near the kitchen door and throw a coat over it. My house-keeping isn't too neat, so no one would even notice it there. I want to go through everything, but my mind is already on overload for the evening.

I go back to the laptop and work on my future webpage for my hunts and try to let everything I have just read percolate in the back of my mind.

I write up thank you letters to print out and mail to all my clients for the moose hunts. This will sure save time. I can personalize each one before printing.

When I write the one to my grandfather, I write it the same as the others and do not admit knowing who he is. He knows where I am and what I do, if he wants further contact with me, he can tell me who he is. I do thank him for the very nice tip.

By the time I am done with the letters, I am ready to shut down the generator for the night. I send a quick message to Grant telling him I am going to shut down and he sends right back to go ahead. Maybe we can make this work.

When I get up this morning, I know it is only a matter of days before I will no longer be able to do any digging or work on foundations, so I start an area to build a new cabin this winter. While I am whacking away with the grub hoe, Grant comes out to see what I am doing. He says it is a good idea and starts shoveling the dirt I am knocking loose over to one side to be used to fill in low spots later, if needed.

As soon as I am worn out, he takes over and soon we have a nice area leveled out better and we can set blocks for the foundation. He suggests we do another one, just in case we have plenty of warm days or at least no wind during the winter for working outdoors. Sounds fine to me.

These two are on the other side of the outhouse from the current cabins. Might as well keep it handy for everyone to use. These two are going to be small, just for overnight stays, and not for living in. More like large solid tents, not even insulated. We measure out for the pier blocks and set them in place. If we can at least have the floor done, it will be easier building the walls on it and standing them up in place on a level surface.

Since these are so small, we actually get both floors done and leveled on the pier blocks. I can see we might get this done.

This morning when I get up, it still isn't snowing, so I take my old truck and head down to the river.

There are some stands of spruce near there that are crowded so badly that they are very tall and straight with few limbs on the lower part. I cut a load of them, limb them and cut to 8 foot lengths. When I limb them, I cut pretty deep, so they won't really need peeled to use as wall studs in the cabins. We will use 2x4s for top and bottom plates and around windows and doors.

Grant slightly bawls me out for going after the poles by myself. I figure since he is still a police officer, even if not actually on duty, it is best if he does not help me acquire poles from state land. I don't tell him my reasons, I just meekly say, "Sorry, wasn't thinking."

We unload near the future cabins and start building walls. I have some T 1-11 on hand, so we nail that to each section before lifting it into place. The walls with a window, we place the window, then the siding and the trim around the window before lifting the wall section and nailing it down. We notch the top of the siding panels to place the rafters down into later so we don't have wide gaps for the bugs and squirrels to go through. Once we have the roof on, the cabin will be weather tight and as soon as a door is installed, it could be camped in.

When I get up this morning it is heavy cloud cover and I am pretty sure our snow free days are about to end. I figure one more trip to town should get all the last minute things we may need. I stop to see if Grant needs anything from town and he wants to go also, so locks up and we head for town.

I pick up some more feed for the animals, just in case and more roofing materials. I find a good sale on windows so get two, one for each cabin. The doors are reasonable, so two of them go on the load also.

I stop and pick up more staple groceries to have on hand. There is no such thing as having too much flour, sugar and salt, but chocolate takes up a good portion, as you can never have even enough of that.

I have the back seat practically filled to the roof when Grant comes out with his shopping. He manages to stuff his bags in and around my load. We tarp and cargo net the load in the pickup. Snow is starting to lazily fall while we are fastening the net.

As we leave city limits, the snow is getting serious and the wind is picking up. This fast trip to town may end up taking a lot longer than I planned.

What took us just over an hour to drive coming in to town ends up taking just over 3 hours to drive, getting home. The road is terrible and the snow is really piling up fast. I am inching along as we head up the last hill before my driveway when we come to a bone jarring halt.

Grant and I both are trying to figure out just what I have hit, when the snow swirls away for a moment and I see the back of a large tractor/trailer unit parked in the road. Neither of us are hurt and the air bags didn't even go off I was going so slow. We both get out of the pickup and keeping one hand on the big rig, we make our way to the front and knock on the cab door.

The driver is happy to see us and that we are okay after hitting him. He didn't even feel it in his cab. He introduces himself, Caleb Inman, and says he just got the latest weather report on his 2 meter. This storm is supposed to last 2 or 3 days at least, maybe more. I ask him if he wants to come spend the storm with us at my place. He is happy to accept.

We go back to the pickup and I ease away from his truck, then up around him and put my emergency flashers on, hoping he can see them better through the storm. He stays so close behind me I figure if I stop, he is going right over the top of me. No wonder I drove the old truck today. It knows the road home. I signal after having turned off the flashers, so he knows which way we are turning.

We both make it into my driveway without hitting the ditch and he parks his truck as far over to the side of the driveway as he can pull it. Grant scoots over and Caleb gets in my pickup and we go over to the cabins. He will stay in the one Jim and Teri were using as it has a heater and is insulated fairly well.

We get him settled in and the fire going in the heater, then unload Grants purchases at his cabin. He rides over to the house with me and helps unload the cab of the truck. The stuff under tarp in the back will be okay until after the storm is over. I take Grant back to his cabin and leave a couple of jars of the meat sauce I canned earlier and a pack of noodles for him to cook for him and Caleb for dinner. I don't think either one is going to want to come out in this weather and walk clear over to my house. Then there would be the walk back after dinner. Nope, not worth it no matter how good a cook I am.

I start up the generator and get the internet going for Grant and then prepare myself some dinner. The bucket of ice cream I put on the porch should stay frozen so I don't even open it tonight. The temperature has been steadily dropping all afternoon and evening and by the time I go to bed, it is minus 23 degrees F. Anuktuvik really doesn't want to stay outside very long when he goes out for the evening walk.

After I eat some dinner, I check out the weather forecast. It does not look good for anyone traveling. At least we didn't see anyone else out on the road today. I send a message to Grant asking how they are doing and he answers right back to let me know they are both doing fine. I tell him if they want to come through the snow tomorrow, I will bake fresh bread so they can have plenty for the next few days. He says he told Caleb and he will definitely be here for fresh baked bread.

I set the sourdough pot to working for the night before I go to bed and Anuktuvik out for one last run.

He comes back in covered in snow and shakes it all over inside the house. I decide to stay up until he is entirely dry as he likes to sleep on the bed, too.

When I wake up this morning, it is very still, the wind isn't blowing at present. I hurry up after filling the stove and setting the bread, and start shoveling the steps and over to the pickup. There is still snow falling, but not like yesterday. I go check my ancient pickup with the snow plow blade on the front. It starts right up and I slowly ease it across the yard, pushing snow as far into the trees as possible, I go back and forth several times to make my yard as clear as possible, then run in to check the bread and punch it down.

I start edging the plow out the main driveway. I angle it so the berm won't build up against the large tractor/trailer unit and keep plowing until I have the driveway twice as wide as usual and the area used to park well cleared back. If I don't keep it as far back as possible, by spring, there won't even be room to drive through.

I plow on the main highway a little bit each direction so maybe when the highway department finally plows through, they won't block me entirely. I finally park the plow facing out and ready to go as this storm is not over, just having a lull. Then I go in and shape the bread into rolls and a couple of loaves and set to raise again.

The men have perfect timing and are coming in the door as I take the pans out of the oven. I have the butter set out and knives, so we make lunch of hot from the oven rolls. I finally remember to set out a jar of blueberry jelly and we each have another for dessert.

The loaves come out of the oven as we are finishing our meal. I set them on racks to cool and will send one over with the men to have as they need it. Probably a jar of the jelly, also. Grant says he has butter. He also has jelly but it is from the store and not half as good as this is.

Caleb figures he better head back to town instead of continuing north after the storm, since he has to leave his vehicle idling or it won't start at these temperatures and he doesn't want to run out of fuel somewhere up north.

By the time they are ready to walk back to the cabins, the wind is picking up again and they are happy there are now berms along the entire driveway. It will be harder to get lost now in the storm. They just have to follow the berms to the cabins. They take their bread and jelly and are happy.

By evening, it is as bad as it was yesterday. If there is a letup in the storm in the morning, I will have to plow again. If it gets too deep, it is more difficult to remove.

Looks like today is a repeat of yesterday except I am not making bread today. Morning brings a bit of calm from the wind and I hurry up and plow. The main road does not look like the road department has made it out. I plow even farther on each side of my driveway, both directions. Even before I finish, the wind is picking up again and the snow is falling heavier.

I park the plow truck and head inside. I guess I am going to have to fill the tanks on the plow truck fairly soon at this rate. Plowing uses a lot of gas.

I bring in as much firewood as I can stack in my wood box and on my porch and still get in and out through the doors. This storm could last several more days and I have used almost all I had inside.

By the time I bring in my last armload of firewood, the wind and snow are howling again. It is surprising how easy it is to get disoriented in this weather. My trail I shoveled out earlier has almost entirely drifted in.

While I am standing in the window, an unfamiliar vehicle pulls up in my yard. What idiot would be driving in this weather on purpose? The storm closes back in and I can't see who is getting out of the vehicle. I grab a handgun and go to the door.

At least they had the good sense to park as close to the door as they could get without making this a drive through. Although if they leave it parked there, no one else can come in or go out that door. The driver hurriedly slams the door as he makes his way up my steps and smacks into the door with an added push from the wind. After some struggle, the outer door comes open and he makes it into the calm on my porch and shuts the door behind him.

I open my inner door as he comes toward it, still holding the gun in my hand behind the door. The person stumbles into my house and drops into the closest chair. "Why would anyone choose to live like this? Why would any sane person live in this place?"

It's a guy. As he slowly unwinds all the gear he has wrapped and draped around himself, I see that it is Jerry, the man that was here with my grandfather. I still have the gun in my hand, out of sight along my leg. The inner door suddenly opens against my back and I realize I have not been too alert.

I jump to the side and bring the gun up, looking back at me is Grant. Oops.

He heard the vehicle and saw a flash of the lights through the snow and followed it over, then had a hard time getting by it onto the steps to come in. Jerry has finally got most of his outer gear off and is standing as close to the stove as possible without injury to himself. His eyes widened at the sight of the gun.

He says when he landed and rented the vehicle, he was advised to only drive it as far as the nearest hotel and stay in the hotel until this storm blew over. Of course he thought they were exaggerating. It's just some snow, right?

He was supposed to come out, invite me to visit Mr. Parnetti and get back to town in time for the evening flight out. Instead, that flight has already gone and he is stuck out here. Who knew an hour trip could take almost 4 hours or more. He says he got stuck in a couple of snow drifts on his way out, the road isn't cleared and what are the highway guys doing? Was I having more problems, since I have a gun in my hand?

Grant and I help him get his gear back on and he will spend the night over in either Grant or Caleb's cabin and have dinner with them. If his vehicle isn't moved soon, it is going to be very hard to get it out without a lot of shoveling.

Chapter 19

Grant takes the keys Jerry hands him and they go out to the vehicle blocking my steps. Grant gets in easily, but it is a chore for Jerry to get off the steps and around the rig.

I watch from my window as Grant turns the rig around and they drive back out to the cabins. That was interesting.

This morning, I catch the early lull in the storm and plow out again. Jerry's rental is still parked over by the cabins. I pull in to see how the men are all doing. Caleb sees me coming and has the door ready to open as soon as I hit the porch. All three men are in Grant's cabin as he is preparing break-fast. I ask him if he has enough supplies and he says yes, he does. Although if my chickens are still laying, maybe some fresh eggs if I have plenty. I do so will have them ready for his next trip over to the house.

Jerry asks if I have an answer for his boss. I do have an answer and it isn't the one he was wanting. There is no way I can leave my home to freeze up and my chickens and pets at any time during the winter. Even a trip to town has to be planned and quick enough not to let the fire go out in the stove.

I give him my email address in case he wants to contact me in the future and save himself a long trip. I tell him I only check it in the evenings, after everything is done for the day and the generator is started. As I leave, he is still muttering about crazy people living like this on purpose.

As I am getting into my plow truck, I hear the highway plow go by, heading toward town, so I go back in to let Caleb and Jerry know, This crew only plows halfway to town, so unless the other crew is also plowing out this way, this only fixes half the trip in. Jerry says that is okay, the worst part was on this side of the top of the highest hill. Caleb decides to head back to town, also, so as soon as they have eaten, they will leave.

The storm is a little slower about starting back up today, so after I park the plow truck, I carry in more wood and shovel a lot of snow away from my steps and walkways.

It is snowing again by evening, but not as hard and the wind has died down to occasional gusts. When I get back on line after dinner, there is a message waiting for me from Jerry. He and Caleb both made the trip to town without much trouble.

Early this morning, I hear a very large vehicle pull in and there is Caleb, smiling down from his cab. He has brought out a bag of fresh fruit as a thank you for being allowed to stay here during the storm. The reports say the storm didn't hit farther north, so he is making another try at delivery of his load. He turns around fairly easily in my yard and heads on north.

I plow again today, and do a very good job on it to make sure we have enough room by spring time. We usually start out with many small snowfalls and it builds up slowly all winter. We already have more snow than I have seen some entire winters.

I fuel up the plow truck and park it back near the house. I like having it handy when I need to plow. I cover the windshield with a tarp and that is my Alaskan portable garage. I already have the new pickup covered that way.

I sweep off the old pickup and start it up to move and unload the load we brought out from town the day the storm started. I clear the berm from my plowing away from the old truck, toss the shovel and a broom on the load and drive over to the cabins. I start out be shoveling a path to the new cabins and then shoveling off the floors. Then I sweep them clear. We can stack the supplies on one and work on the other one.

Grant comes hurrying out pulling on his mitts as I start undoing the cover over the load. We unload the truck and put the doors in on the walls we have up for them. No roof, but we can lock the door. The walls for the big windows are ready for them, also. Big being a relative term, but large enough to qualify as egress windows in a very small cabin. There is a small window in each cabin, for a cross breeze if they are open. Each door has a small window in it also, so anyone using the cabin can see out if they want to check for bears before opening the door. Only the side next to the other cabin doesn't have a window. Seems more private that way.

We build gable ends and place them at each end over the door and opposite. Then we use a peeled pole as a ridgepole and start on rafters. They slide in the slots I have cut for them and the birds mouth locks them in place while we nail them down. This cabin is ready to put the nailers across and the roofing on, next time we work on it. We have worked hard enough neither of us has felt the cold all day.

As we are walking back out from the cabin, the cold starts being noticeable. The temperature is dropping fairly fast so I say goodnight and thanks for the help and drive my old truck back to park it at home. I cover it the same as the others and am very happy to get indoors.

This morning, the thermometer is hovering at minus 32 degrees F. I think it is an excellent day to stay indoors and maybe do some baking.

I check the chickens in their coop and it is getting enough warmth from the vent into the house to stay above freezing. It isn't warm, but certainly not as cold as outside. The eggs roll from the nest boxes into a box in the house through the vent area I made. I make sure they have water and plenty of feed and grit.

Anuktuvik and Kivalina are very happy to have me in the house all day. They stay underfoot all the time I am making bread and later, they are still underfoot as I start a large pot of beans soaking. I like having beans or stew ready in case anyone is hungry when the weather is like this. It is comfort food for me. The fresh hot bread adds the final touch to that.

After I drain and rinse the beans a couple of times and bring them back to a boil, I put them on the wood heater to simmer along all afternoon. I add lots of onion, celery, diced carrots and garlic to the beans and the house smells very good. Then the bread and rolls add aroma to it and I am feeling starved.

The breeze must be blowing the right direction because Grant comes to the door just as the rolls come out of the oven. I have made a small pan of caramel rolls and those are ready to take out of the oven, also. Then the loaves go in.

I set the sweet rolls on the counter with the butter and we both have dessert first. We talk a while then have a roll and a bowl of beans. When the loaves are done, I set one on the porch and it cools very fast so I can wrap it for Grant to take back to his cabin with him.

The cold weather appears to be here to stay a while, so I start in on the bear rugs from the spring bear hunts. I picked them up from the tannery our last trip to town. I write the owners name in magic marker inside each one so after I remove the metal locking tags I can still tell who has which bear.

While looking through my paperwork, I notice several clients also listed email addresses. I enter them in my address book on-line when I go on so I can update them on the progress of their bears and ask for approval on color combinations for the backing. I like to double check because once in a while after the client gets home and talks to his wife, she does not want the colors he chose in her house.

After another bowl of beans I start up the generator for the evening internet. I write up a letter to use as the base for inquiries about hunts, another for rug information for successful clients that contracted me to make rugs for them. After entering the email addresses I located earlier, I am almost done for the evening when I decide to actually check my email.

I have one from Jerry back home wherever he lives. He tells me Mr. Parnetti is disappointed that I won't join him for the holidays. I write back that I am sorry but winter is not a time of year that I can leave my home, with wood heat and no electricity, I would lose everything including my pets and chickens. I told him all of this while he was here, but tell him yet again. Maybe he needs it in hard copy to show his boss.

I message Grant to let him know I am shutting everything off. He asks for a few more minutes, he is in the middle of something so I tell him to let me know when he is ready. I doze off while waiting and almost fall off my chair which wakes me up enough to see his message waiting. I shut down and go to bed. Then, of course, I am wide awake.

After a night of tossing and turning, I am not ready when morning hits. I am also not ready when

Grant shows up at my door to see if I would like to ride along with him to town as he has to go in and phone in a report. They are not happy with only internet in the evening reporting from him. I say sure, why not? and load up the stove with firewood and send Anuktuvik out for a run before we go. I make us each a sandwich to eat on the way from thick slices of homemade bread and some leftover meatloaf I have on hand. I fill a couple of drink containers from the cooler and I am ready to go when Grant pulls over in his pickup.

The roads have been cleared very well and it is a fairly quick trip to town. Not as quick as in the summer, but for winter, a quick trip. He drops me off at the member warehouse store and he goes on over to turn in his verbal report and whatever he has written up.

I didn't think I needed anything, but by the time he gets back, I have a very large cart filled. Now that it is dependably cold, I can keep frozen foods the rest of the winter so I am loading up on vegetables and fruit, already frozen. I even find some meats marked down that can be frozen to change the diet this winter. I have some of the #10 cans of dehydrated food, also, for changing some recipes and adding flavor. I may not have needed anything but I have managed to just spend quite a bit of money on things I really could have made the winter without.

We load everything into the pickup and fuel up. Then we stop at the truck stop on the way home for something to eat. The sandwiches were many hours ago.

By now we need to be getting back home so the houses don't freeze up. We see a couple of moose along the road on our way home. The early deep snow is going to be rough on them this winter. Especially the young ones. Even worse is the special cow season that drags on into December. The poor cows are already stressed with winter and early pregnancy, and have to look out for getting shot in the only areas cleared of snow, along the roadways is just one extra stress too many. Yeah, I know, I'm a hunter and also make a living from hunting by guiding, but I certainly do not agree with killing off the cows.

The wind has drifted some snow across my driveway, but the pickup plows right on through it with no problems. There is still a faint plume of smoke from my chimney as we pull up by my door so that is nice. The warmth inside as I open the door is lovely.

Anuktuvik stops long enough for a quick pet on his way out the door. I pull the generator out to it's little cubby off the porch and start it up so we have lights to finish unloading and bring in another large box of frozen vegetables to store on the porch. I start loading wood into the stove and open the damper and drafts wide open to make sure it catches well as low as it was. Grant unloads the rest of my boxes of groceries and goes back over to his cabin. It has been a long busy day.

When I plop down in a chair, I find it is hard to motivate myself enough to get back up out of it. A trip to town is worse than a full day of working here building a cabin. I am worn out.

I work a while on the bear rugs. At present, I am doing all the heads and have one head finished and the rug stretched out and drying, nailed down to my floor. Someday, I will build another room onto the house to use for this. Then my house won't always have bears laying around in it in various stages of undress.

I message Grant that I am shutting off and no answer so I go ahead and do it. I need some sleep.

It is fairly nice for this time of year, so I gather up some boards to use as nailers across the rafters and load them in the back of the old pickup to haul over to the cabin work site.

It is a bit clumsier to work wearing cold weather gear, but not impossible. Once you get the hang of it, the work progresses quite well. Ladders are a challenge, but for me they always are anyway. We have a love/hate relationship, I hate them and they love to dump me.

Grant comes out while I am unloading the truck and starts helping. Then we get the nailers fastened down on the rafters and start on the roofing. This is the tricky part in the cold. I am putting metal roofing on the cabins and it is very slick when icy.

Since these are small cabins, we can reach most of each sheet of metal from the ladder inside the cabin and work both sides as we go so we can also do the top. We probably won't get the ridge cap on now as neither of us wants to climb on the metal. The building may have some leaking directly down the ridge seam, but that shouldn't be as bad as the entire roof not being on all winter.

We manage to get the small roof done today and that is great. If the weather is this 'warm' tomorrow, we will be back building walls for the other one to finish it. We have most of it done, just 1 more wall and the gable ends to go.

After dinner, I work on the rugs some more. I would like to have some ready to mail out on the next trip to town. This evening I add the fabric backing, padded with quilt filling, then edged with a ruffle all around in two colors of polar fleece. It doesn't ravel and is soft, yet doesn't crush like felt, which is used traditionally, does. This makes these rugs something that can be used as a throw over a couch or a bed. They are soft and warm and all you have to do is be careful not to thunk someone with the head.

I have made up a standard email to let clients know when their rug is ready and how much the final cost will be and the rug will be shipped upon receiving the balance due. Sometimes I haul a rug already boxed for shipping back and forth a few times before I receive the balance due. Now I can nudge the ones I have email addresses for, about the rugs. I always take a nice photo to attach to the email, so they can see how their rug looks.

Chapter 20

Halloween has come and gone and guess what? Not a single trick or treater comes to my door. No one pulls any stupid pranks on me either. Just one more perk of living out in the middle of nowhere.

Grant has finally told me he is writing a book. He was involved in a large scale drug bust a couple of years ago on the Border and wants to tell it but as fiction. His ideas sound very interesting and he has asked me to proof read it for him. Sure, I will read anything. Especially by the end of winter.

We have the second little cabin enclosed now with the roof on it, the same as the other one. I may insulate the ceilings later, as I can, so they will be a bit more comfortable than tents in very hot weather. Yes, Alaska can have some very hot weather in the summer, it happens.

I have most of the rugs done now and several of the clients have said they sent the final checks, so I will need to make a trip to town If the checks are in, most of the clients will have their rugs by Christmas.

. I still haven't used the new truck for a town trip

and hesitate to do so now. I can just see getting it's first dent. Maybe when clients start showing up in the spring for the spring bear hunts. The roads should all be clear by then.

I load all the packed up rugs into the old pickup and ask Grant if he wants a ride to town. He says he is more than ready for a break and will go. We will leave very early in the morning and hope to be home in the middle of the afternoon. Neither end of the trip will be in daylight. We are down to less than 4 hours per day for possible sunlight. On the Winter Solstice, we have about an hour less sunlight than Fairbanks as we are closer to the Arctic Circle.

The morning trip is uneventful and there actually are several checks waiting for me in my mailbox. I deposit them and pull out enough to mail the packages for the ones that paid.

Then I pick up a few items to have for Christmas. Grant fills up the fuel polydrums in the back of the truck for the generators and we head for home.

On our way home, Grant tells me he called to see how Cary and Sheila are doing. Sheila is out of her coma but has huge blanks in her memory or is an extremely good actress. She is considered stable enough to send back to Texas to continue recovery but she doesn't want to go.

Cary is still not doing very well, but is talking a lot and evidently about many things he may wish later he had kept quiet about. No real evidence, just hints and a few remarks, when added to others, make sense.

We did well today. It isn't even fully dark when we get home. We unload the polydrums in the gas shed and lock it up. Then we unload the rest of the stuff. Grant didn't buy much, except the fuel and some snack items.

Jeff stops by on his swing north on patrol and says Sheila has asked if she can come out here to recuperate. Oh heck no. I've had more than enough of that whole group. I leave no doubt in Jeff's mind on how I feel about that suggestion. It's been rather nice not having shots fired, buildings broken into and fires started, even small explosions. I really don't need nor want any more of that.

His next trip out, he stops and hands me a note Sheila wrote. I guess she really isn't used to being told no. I write a quick note on the bottom of hers and send it on with him. I firmly and emphatically say no.

I invited Jim, Teri, Jeff and Grant over to my place for Christmas. I get an email back from Teri, Sheila is temporarily staying with her and can she bring her out with them, just for the holiday. Sunofagun. She's going to get here one way or another.

I email Teri and ask if she has had any fires, explosions or stray gunshots lately. She writes back that, no, she hasn't had any. Okay, then, bring her along but she goes back with them.

Since none of us have family in Alaska, we will be our own family for this holiday. Even Sheila and she actually does have family with Cary still here. They show up the day before Christmas. Jim and Jeff will stay with Grant, Teri and Sheila will share the other cabin that has a stove. Grant started the fire in it early this morning so the mattresses have time to warm, also. I have been baking for a couple of days, so there is pie as soon as they get here. Jeff will be here later after he gets off shift tonight.

I have a fake tree set up and all the bear parts and hides out of the way for Christmas. My home looks pretty good by propane light. I have the wall lamps lit, instead of any lanterns. The lanterns are too bright and noisy.

We soon relax and it is just like when they were here before. Even Sheila relaxes and says she understands why I don't want her staying here long term.

They go get settled into their cabins and come back over to spend the afternoon. We actually all have a very good time and by the time Jeff shows up, dinner is ready. Jeff is really hungry, the rest of us, not so much. We have been eating on desserts, candy and cookies I made, all afternoon while we talked.

I think he caught up on the sweets after dinner. I hope his stomach can handle all of that just before bedtime. I turn off all the lights except the one in the kitchen and start the generator. The tree lights are the only electric lights on in the house.

After we all wind down and are ready to call it a night, they all bundle up to walk back to their cabins. The aurora is putting on an amazing light show for us, overhead, with a huge coronal arc directly overhead. I grab a coat and stand to watch it with them. No one wants to walk away and miss some of the show. Finally I have to go back inside, I didn't put outdoor boots on and the parka only goes so far keeping me warm without boots, just my house slippers. Lucky for me, they are fur, so not as bad as it sounds.

Sheila and Grant have never seen the aurora like this before so they are gently guided along toward the cabins while trying to not lose a minute of watching the sky. After they get in their cabins, they go sit in windows and continue watching in comfort until the lights slowly fade away.

Overhead aurora

Chapter 21

None of them is as bad as small children, but it is still very early when they all arrive back at my house. I had placed stockings for each one along the shelf behind my stove as I didn't think my pets would behave themselves all that well if placed in easy reach.

To say they are surprised is an understatement. Sheila starts to cry and I haven't a clue what to do. Luckily Teri seems to know more about this sort of stuff and hugs her and lets her cry. Then when she stops, she flings herself into my arms and I manage not to either deck her or dodge out of the way.

I'm feeling rather proud of myself for not doing either. She finally lets go and steps back, saying she is sorry. It is the first Christmas stocking she has ever gotten in her entire life. Aw geez.

I offer everyone some pie before we start opening presents and they are surprised but willing. Pie is enjoyed far more before everyone is overstuffed from dinner.

I made trapper hats for each of the guys from scraps left over on bear fur from making the rugs. They look like wild mountain men. For the women, I used fox fur, not as wild looking and still very warm.

They are all grinning like crazy when they hand me

an envelope. Inside is a voucher to help install the foam board insulation they banded together and brought out for the 2 little cabins. Now it is my turn to feel like just maybe I want to allow a tear or two. I successfully fight the feeling and we continue opening some humorous presents everyone managed to find for each person. I have a French toast casserole in the oven and soon we are sitting around enjoying a hot breakfast and the good fire. I start a nice large turkey roasting after breakfast and we laze around talking and playing some old board games I have on hand.

We have less than three hours of sunlight today, but we enjoy every one of them. It's not all that cold and no wind, so we actually go over and insulate one of the cabins.

When we come back to the house, the smell of dinner cooking is so good, we all get right in and finish preparing it and prepare to sit down to eat a bit early.

We haven't even started dinner and someone drives into my yard. Anuktuvik is at attention but not growling.

I can't believe it. It is Jerry and Joe, my probable grandfather.

I invite them in and Teri is setting 2 more places at the table. No matter what it is, we all have to eat and I'm not letting this dinner get cold before I even taste it. I really enjoy my food and Christmas dinner is one of the best times for really good food. Teri brought out some delicious family favorites, Grant fixed a few he really likes and Jim and Jeff both added some dishes to today's feast. The table is filled with good food, let's eat.

Jerry and Joe are a bit uncomfortable at first, just coming in and starting to eat. Soon they have relaxed and are enjoying dinner as much as the rest of us are. I'm not sure why they are here but we all enjoy the meal and sit around visiting after. Jeff says he has to get back to town this evening, he has a shift in the morning. Jim and Teri both have to be at work tomorrow afternoon, so they all decide to leave at the same time to make sure both vehicles make it to town okay. Personally, I think they were freeing up the other warm cabin for these two to spend the night.

Grant leaves when the rest do, and says he will be back in an hour or so. He knows who Joe is, and wants to give us some privacy to get acquainted. I am having a hard time making the leap from Joe the client to Joe = Grandpa, right here, in my house, right now.

I ask if they have had a good trip coming up and they both say yes. Now what? That was the only thing I could think of to say and now I am stumped, so I ask if they will be spending the night, I have a warm cabin they can use.

Finally Joe asks if I know that he is my grandfather? I tell him yes, but didn't want to presume on that in case he wasn't prepared to have me as his granddaughter. That I had looked him up on the internet after Grant got it installed out here.

He says internet is a wonderful thing, it is how he finally found his daughter after so many years wasted, only to learn she had died. He had stalled a bit right there until later, he read a bit further, and found she was survived by a daughter. He says he didn't know how to raise a daughter and he has no idea how to be a grandfather., but he would like to be involved in my life.

I tell him that after the driver brought the pickup here and said my grandfather gave it to me, I had looked him up, also on the internet. He looked a bit uncomfortable about that and said he hoped I didn't believe everything I read on-line.

I told him I believe nothing I hear or read and only part of what I see. He says that is a good philosophy.

Grant comes back over and knocks before coming in. I ask if anyone wants more pie or any of the rest of dinner, then start putting food away. We all have one more piece of pie and resume talking.

He asks a lot of questions about my Mom and if she was happy. I truly believe she was and I know my parents loved each other. To lose them at the same time was very hard on me, but that is how they would have wanted it, if given a choice.

I tell him all I remember about our life together while they were still alive. By the time I could remember much, we were living at the Roadhouse. To me, it was a wonderful place, full of odd nooks and crannies indoors and out. Since it had been there from Gold Rush days, there was a lot of stuff accumulated in the outbuildings. Harnesses for dogs and horses still hung on pegs in the old barn. Hand tools for building, cutting hay and other chores lined the walls. I still owned the remains of the property but had been unable to rebuild the Roadhouse as it was not insured.

We suddenly realize it is well after midnight and Grant offers to show the men where the other cabin is and he has made sure the fire is still going in the heater. Teri changed the sheets on the beds before she left.

They did not expect to spend the night but there is no reason for them to drive back to town this late at night and they planned on coming back tomorrow anyway.

Chapter 21

Morning comes way too soon. It isn't daylight or even very close to it, but I figure the men are not only still on a different time zone yet and that they want to talk and leave. I can't picture either one of them enjoying winter in Alaska.

So I am very surprised when they show up and ask about renting the cabin for a month. A month? Now? It is almost January and January is not usually much of a tourist month here. Yes, the daylight is now increasing a few minutes a day, but not that much and not any warmth in the sun we do get to see.

At least we don't have it as bad as up at Barrow. They finally get to see the sun again on January 22 after 65 days of no sun. It gets bright for a couple of hours in the middle of the day, but the sun never peeks over the horizon.

I guess if they really don't like it, they can always drive back to town at any time and fly home. I feel bad charging my Grandfather rent. I tell him that and he laughs a sort of rusty laugh like it doesn't get used very often and says he would be paying anywhere he was staying and would rather pay me. I ask if they have enough winter gear and then I wonder about firewood. So far, the other cabin has been using from what Grant bought last fall. I will need to buy some or start cutting some for them to use and to replace Grants. As I think it over, I don't know anyone selling firewood near here, during the winter, so cutting it is my best option. No one from town will deliver now at a reasonable price.

Jerry thinks he picked up enough winter gear for them and used what he learned on his last trip up to make sure he got the right items.

I am still working on the last couple of bear rugs, so while we talk, I work on rugs. I have cleaned the skulls on their bull moose and they are hanging outside on the gable of my roof. I oiled the antlers so they won't weather but the weather does a fine job on the bone. I show them the antlers and they are of the opinion that they look really good right where they are. They have the memories and photos and they take up a lot less room.

They have a point there and if they have small apartments, once the antlers are in it, there may not be room for much else. I can see trying to fit them in a taxi from the airport.

I liked Joe in hunt camp and I find as we spend more time together, that I like him as a Grampa, also. He seems to be a really nice man. Of course, we are getting acquainted as adults and probably a lot different than what my Mom described in her diary. I haven't told Grampa about the diary and not sure I will or even should. She never actually said she understood anything he did or forgave him and it might hurt him more to read a lot of what she did say. I better keep it to myself. No reason to hurt him, I don't know him well enough yet.

I go out fairly early and cut a load of firewood and drop it off near Grant's woodshed. At least that will help on the wood use from what he paid for.

We manage to insulate the inside of the other little cabin and now we pray no weather makes it leak inside before we get a ridge cap on the roofs. It really won't hurt the foam board, but it might make the walls harder to dry out from using green poles. I think Grampa actually enjoyed himself bundling up and working in the winter weather. I take a lot of pictures of him working on the cabin, wearing his parka, heavy mitts and boots. I don't have many family pictures as most of mine were lost in the fire with my folks.

They usually stay at my place until after dinner and then Jerry checks his email to see how things are going back home. Tonight, he acts agitated about something after he is on-line a while and then after doing a few searches, he shuts his laptop down and joins us in conversation for a while. He excuses them early to go back to the cabin. Grampa looks at him but doesn't disagree, and they leave earlier than usual.

This morning, they are gone with a note left on the door, saying they have gone to town to take care of some business and will be back later tonight. I stoke up their fire and go back to my house.

About noon, I decide I need some warm

homemade bread so start a batch. I am just taking it out of the oven when they pull in. Grant has walked over, so they all have perfect timing.

Just coming in to hot bread seems to have relaxed them and they all sit down and start filling up on bread and melting butter with some jelly once in a while.

They also did some grocery shopping while in town and brought out more fresh vegetables and fruit.

This morning, the temperatures have dropped, really dropped. We have been staying in the minus 20's F. but now it drops down into the minus 50's in town. I am lucky that living up here on a hill, it isn't as cold as town or in the valleys, we only get into the minus 30's. Still too cold to be starting up a vehicle without additional warmth for a while. I always make sure there is synthetic oil in mine for the winter. It stays fluid instead of turning solid in extreme cold. But I still don't like starting it at really cold temperatures. So when Jerry comes over to see about getting a ride to town since they managed to kill the battery in their rental, I am not too thrilled with the idea.

A medical emergency, I would, anything else isn't an emergency to me. I tell him I will start up the generator so he can use the internet if it is something he can do that way, but unless someone is having a heart attack or bleeding profusely, no, not going to town.

He and Grampa both walk over, well bundled up,

a short while later and they pull the gift pickup thing on me, so I hand over the title after signing it and the keys ands say, "Have at it. It only has a couple more miles on it than it did when it was delivered."

They stand there in stunned silence a minute or two, then both start to say something, then stop again. Finally, "Why haven't you used it?"

"I was saving it to use with clients and as a good vehicle. My old truck is my work truck. Pretty much like having good clothes for going to town and work clothes. Besides, being from the Anchorage area, it would not be winterized for the Interior weather. One other thing, a gift is a gift, not a weapon to hang over someone's head and used like a club. Keep it"

I stomp back into my bedroom and leave them standing at the door. In a couple of minutes I hear them trying to start the new pickup and the battery promptly dies on it also. It's probably a good thing I started locking my old trucks after the other troubles we were having earlier so no one can easily change out batteries.

They come back to the house and politely knock on the door. They have to be getting cold by now, but they are still determined to get to town. They do finally get it that I am not ruining my vehicles just for them to go to town, so they either need to convince me it is important or they better do it by internet. They decide to try doing it by internet.

I take my generator out and start it, then turn on the internet for them. Only a few minutes after getting on line and they are both sighing in relief, seems the terribly important reason to go to town wasn't that important after all. They usually aren't, unless it does involve heart attacks or excessive bleeding. Those are important, but usually too late by the time they reach town anyway.

However, this episode has put a little distance between me and Grampa. I don't like feeling manipulated or that I am owing someone for something I didn't ask for. I can see where he and my Mom would have had a hard time together.

The cold lasts almost two weeks and Jerry and Grampa are more than ready to go home, I am thinking. They finally ask if I have a battery charger and if I would charge up the battery for their rental if they bring it over. I tell them sure, I will charge it. They bring the battery then go get the one out of the pickup and bring them both in. I charge the rental battery first that night when I run the generator. Mostly, both batteries need to be warmed up, so they charge fairly fast.

The first day it hits only minus 20 degrees F. The battery is back in the pickup and rental and they are packed and ready to go. They even cleaned up the cabin they have been staying in. When I go check it after they leave, I find a letter from Grampa and the title and keys for the pickup.

Now what am I supposed to do with the pickup? I don't think I want to even use it at all. If I use it, will he think he owns me? I just don't like that feeling.

I open the letter after I get back to my house. Grampa is apologizing for the upset and misunderstanding and hopes to keep in touch. Somehow, I don't think the apology comes easy for him. I won't hold hard feelings, but I will be very careful in future dealings with him. No matter what, he is apparently the only family I have.

Grant comes over that evening while the generator is on and asks if he can check the browsing history in my computer to see what was so important for Grampa and Jerry. I am ambivalent about letting him search. This is my Grampa after all. Besides, most of the time, they used Jerry's laptop. Only that last attempt at getting to town and finally checking on-line was done from mine.

After he pulls up the history, it looks like Jerry just checked some newspapers. Grant takes notes for the dates and papers and will go back to his cabin to check on what they were reading. After he leaves, I pull up the back issues they were checking out and don't see anything of interest. Guess that is why I am not a detective.

I'm thinking maybe Jerry checked his email also, while he was on line and then the newspapers Oh well, it's not like I know his email password anyway. Later, when I check mine, I have a message letting me know they arrived home okay. I respond, thanking them, for the visit.

When Grant comes over, I flat ask him if he is investigating my grandfather. I thought he was looking into the death of William Garrison The

Third or did he think my grandfather had anything to do with that?

He looks uncomfortable then says my grandfather was just a bonus, he didn't think he actually had anything to do with anything that happened up here or with William Garrison The Third. Since they were all from Texas or had Las Vegas interests, he just wanted to check them all out while he was here and so were they. He never really believed in coincidences. He may just have found one.

I tell him I think my grandfather actually lives in Arizona. He moved there from Texas almost 20 years ago. Maybe he still owned land in Texas though. He said he went back often to visit friends. He said he had investments in Vegas but certainly didn't want to live there.

The groundhog lies to us yet again about how much winter is left. February passes in a semi-blur. I finish up all the taxidermy projects I have yet to be paid for and have them all packed and ready to ship as soon as I receive payment.

March wanders in and I start cutting down trees to cut up later for firewood. The sap is still down and they are fairly dry and lighter than they will be later in the spring or summer. I also like to get them down before birds start nesting. I hate to find the remains of a nest in a fallen tree. By the first day of spring, we have gained about 8 1/2 hours of sunlight per day so it is easy to get more done outdoors.

I haul my extension ladder over to the small new

cabins and manage to knock most of the snow off without any damage to myself or the roofs. Maybe, just maybe, we can get the ridge caps on soon. Grant comes over as I am about to take the ladder down and asks why we don't just put the caps on now, from the ladder and only screw both ends down, we can get the rest after it dries out. Sounds like a plan to me . We stitch screw 2 lengths of cap together and then walk it up the ladders we now have placed at each end. We do it without any injuries to either of us.

   Grant says he is coming along very well on his book and the winter has been a great success for him having time to do his writing. Yeah, right, he stops and helps whenever I am doing anything around here.

Chapter 22

By the end of March, I have dragged the gear out of the shed and going through it to make sure there is no squirrel or vole damage to anything. It is all over my living room. I can start placing my bait stations the middle of April, but I need to confirm where the best places will be this year for my camps. I try not to overuse any one area so I rotate my camps to several different areas in my game management units.

This year I will set up camp closer to home than I did last year. There was a lot of bear activity around here all summer and I would prefer to never have to shoot one in my yard. I would really prefer to never have to shoot one. A paying client shooting one is a whole different story.

I have an area in mind to set up this years camp, so go up to check it out. As I slog through the snow, it looks like a very good spot for a camp. Access is easy yet not visible from the main road. There is an area I can park my vehicle and not be seen from the road also.

I walk a bit around the part I would like to actually set the camp in and I won't even have to clear any brush. It is a nice open area with a lot of birch around it for shade later in the season yet open enough to have a lot of sun at the present. I tie a few flags of surveyors tape around to make sure I find the same area when I come back. I know the area below here and there are some perfect game trails and areas bears really like. I find the flags I put out last year when I checked this out and it still looks good to me.

The baits will be over a mile from the road and more than a mile from any camp area or home. I prefer them as far as possible yet easy to get to, from any place bears could cause a problem. These baits will be well over 5 miles from any dwelling and that dwelling is mine.

One area I pick is perfect for a tree stand and I will be dragging lumber and plywood over later to build a decent sturdy stand in the trees. I don't want any flimsy stand that can cause accidents. I should have built it last summer but somehow kept getting distracted by other things.

The second bait station I decide on looked perfect last fall but doesn't look as good right now. Maybe it will improve after the snow is all gone. Not that the snow looks like it is going to leave any time soon. We have another small snow storm hit the first day of April. I guess that is our April Fools joke. I am not laughing as I slog through even deeper snow trying to get a nice camp set up.

While working on the bait station, all the snow came off the spruce tree I was working near and completely engulfed me, knocking off my hat, going down the neck of my shirt and into my boot tops, even managing to get inside my pants so I am wet, cold and not in a very good mood when I finally make it home. Talk about someone looking like something the cat drug in, whatever it was, it probably looked better than I do right now.

There is an unfamiliar SUV parked near my house and Grant is standing outside talking to a couple of people I have never seen before. I try to drive right on by but everyone starts waving and trying to stop me, so rather than just run them over, I stop.

As I roll down my window, I must look a sight. My hair is hanging in wet tangles around my face and straggling down my chest and back. My clothes are soggy and I squish when I move. My teeth are chattering and I can feel hypothermia settling in even with my heater cranked on high.

One of the people with Grant is a very chic looking woman that would never be caught dead looking like I do right now in public and the person behind her aiming a large camcorder over her, right at me, is looking to get killed.

I must not look too friendly or my intent is showing on my face as Grant steps in front of the camera guy and puts a hand over the lens. He holds up his other hand and the guy stops muttering and actually takes a look at me. "Oh, right," he mutters, "Let her get cleaned up a bit first."

I put the pickup in gear and start easing away from them on over to my house. They are walking along behind but I am in the house and the door is locked before they make it to my porch.

Grant tries the door and then turns and talks to the couple behind him a bit while I try to stop my teeth chattering long enough to change clothes and get my hair wrapped in a towel and off my face and back. Just getting dry clothes on helps and I heat some water to get some hot chocolate made and drank before I feel up to even trying to see what the other people want. A camera? This can't be good.

Grant taps on the door again and I can see the other two out in the yard, so I go let him in. When he comes in, he is very subdued and is having trouble telling me whatever it is, so it must mean something has happened to someone I know.

"Oh, just tell me. The suspense is getting me thinking it is the worst thing that could happen."

"Well, someone tried to blow up your grandfather. He is mostly okay, but they have him at the hospital near his home trying to keep him safe."

"Mostly? How bad is mostly?"

"Kelly, I don't know, these two showed up and told me, so that is all I know. They want to interview you."

"For what? It's not like I really know the man."

Grant goes out and brings them in. By this time the woman is shivering a bit and trying not to show it. I hand her one of the blankets I have warming by the stove and wrap it over her shoulders. I am bundled into one also, so we hover over the stove and shiver into our blankets.

She asks me how I got so wet this time of year and I give her a rundown on my day. She has the good grace to apologize for waylaying me in the driveway.

I tell her I was trying to get home before hypothermia made me unable to drive. It was darn cold being so wet in this weather. The wind made it even worse. She could only imagine how I felt being so wet as she was freezing and wasn't even damp.

While we are still bundled near the fire, I ask her in a low voice what she heard about my grandfather.

She tells me only that she was sent out to see how I was reacting to the news of his being injured. I said until they told us, I didn't know he had been and still know nothing more than what they have said.

For the first time, she realizes there are no phones here. Cell service is nonexistent. She alone is telling me the news and she is uncomfortable with that. She must be new to being a reporter. I tell her I never even met the man until last fall on a hunt and didn't know he was my grandfather until after he left. She is incredulous. "You mean you are related to one of the richest men in the country and didn't even know it?"

"What? He is what?"

I plop back down on the block of wood I was sitting on and sit there in stunned silence. Grant comes over and asks if everything is okay. No, no it isn't.

When I thought he was just a nice old man and

maybe I could help him out, that was okay, but a rich old man? No, that is just not the way things go. Yes, he bought me a pickup and yes, they are very expensive, and yes, he hired someone to drive it up here, but I just thought maybe he had a good retirement program or something.

With government agents watching him, he might not have all that money for long, if they can tie him in to anything illegal. I know they have been trying. Sometimes I think Grant is out here keeping an eye on me to see if I am tied into any of the doings going on with the rest of the mess. If nothing else, it does make me feel a bit safer having him staying out here.

I finally get my hair dry and braid it off my face. The hot chocolate has warmed me up on the inside a bit and maybe the sugar helped out some, also. The reporter is looking better after hers, also. Grant and the camera man are fine with just having something to drink. Neither one was suffering as far as I could tell. I ask the reporter who sent her out this far wearing town clothes?

She looks daggers at her camera man and says he said it would be okay, just from the warm car to a warm house and back. Yeah, like anyone that has lived up here very long would go this far from town dressed in a dress and nice shoes. I ask him if this is his first winter up here also and he says yes, how did I know? Some things are obvious.

I convince them there really isn't any story here, and they eventually go. I ask Grant to please tell me just what everyone else seems to know or think they know about my grandfather. He hems and haws around and finally tells me it has been suspected over the years that my grandfather was some sort of financial wizard with gambling casinos and money.

It appeared he was good enough at gambling to make a really decent living at it, and beyond a decent living, actually, he got very wealthy at it. He always declared it and paid taxes on it and no one could find out if or how he was doing it. Some thought he was actually laundering money for mob connections, but he never associated with any type of underworld characters. He was a private person and didn't party or keep a mistress, so there was no way to trap him that way.

I asked if just possibly he maybe was on the up and up?

Grant said he just didn't know. The mess with William Garrison The Third came along about the time they were looking into Joe's affairs and they found that The Third was an innocent victim with his Assistant, John McCready actually running the money laundering through his casinos in Vegas. My grandfather was vaguely acquainted with both of them, having met in passing in Vegas. There was no sign that they actually knew each other, but the Feds were really trying to find a link. Innuendo and rumor were hacking a lot of reputations to shreds over the whole thing.

He said he really shouldn't be telling me any of this, but if I was going to be getting blindsided by reporters over it, I should at least know a bit of what they were talking about. He personally thought some of the Feds were leaking the info to fuel the rumors and keep their jobs going. Several of them enjoyed being in Vegas, undercover.

That night I have an email from Jerry, telling me about my grandfather and that he is okay. More shook up than injured.

I answer back and thank him for telling me and letting him know that the reporters had been out here earlier about it.

Grant stayed long enough to share a small evening meal with me and make sure I really feel okay and then went back to his cabin to check and see what he could find through his contacts. Just as I am about to stop for the night, I get a message from Grant and he says he found a few things on line I might be interested in. I tell him to come on over or I won't get any sleep tonight wondering.

He is soon at my door and has his laptop. He sets it up and brings up some news articles he has found. I start reading and they are interesting but I am not making any connections here. Yeah, I am so not a detective.

Grant starts pointing out little pieces of each story and saves them over to one side until they are actually making sense to me, even. Most of the articles are about The Third and his various enterprises. His marriage to Sheila and her brother Cary entering in as someone on the edges of their society.

Then he goes deeper into Cary and Sheila's past and has their parents getting married when Cary was almost a teen and Sheila was a very young girl. So he really was a brother, an older stepbrother. There were even a couple of pictures and she was always looking up at her older brother, hero worship in her eyes.

Cary had some problems growing up and got in some trouble but the records were sealed on those. He seemed to get it together after he grew up or got better at being bad and not getting caught.

I never do see the link with my grandfather though. They were all in Vegas once at the same time, but there were a whole lot of other people there at the same time, too. I think they are really stretching it. The President was in Vegas, is he a suspect too? Grant doesn't see the humor in that.

He leaves soon after and I shut down the generator, fuel up the stove and go to bed.

The weather has not improved. So much for global warming, personally, I am looking at the horizon for the oncoming glaciers of the next ice age. It is cold and there is some snow falling off and on all morning. I decide to stay in and do some baking. I need some bread for sandwiches anyway.

While I am at it, I check the frozen food on my porch and bring some in to start cooking so I can process it this afternoon. I will use more of it for the next few days as my meals so nothing thaws out and is wasted. My freezer is about to become a cool room, I hope. Even if it isn't in any big hurry to do that. Maybe if I left all that expensive food out there, it would warm up? Not going to waste food to find out.

While the meat is cooking and the bread dough is rising, I actually start doing some cleaning. Once hunting season gets here and I start taking clients out to hunt camp, nothing is going to get done around here. I have set up a feeder for the chickens that holds over a weeks worth of food and the same for a waterer for them. I get a huge tote to use as a litter box for Kivalina and find bulk feeder and water containers for her, also.

Anuktuvik will probably come with me although when I go out with a client, he will have to be shut in the truck. I will enjoy having him in camp with me the rest of the time, though. Having him in the tent with me while I sleep will certainly let me know if bears or anything else is in the area.

The weather is making it difficult to get my camp set up. I am certainly glad it is not all that far from home this year. I have managed to drag a large cross bed toolbox in and have the tents and sleeping bags stored in it, away from the weather and small rodents. I finally complete my tree stand and have a decent ground stand set up, in a nice location farther up the valley.

The season to hunt bears over bait starts April 15th, so it isn't only a bad day for taxpayers. I don't book any hunts to start until May 1st. Our weather usually is so rotten in April that not only would the hunters be miserable, the bears take one look and stay in their dens, usually. I prefer to have happy clients and to actually get what they are paying to be here for.

We still have some snow on the ground when I go in to pick up my first clients of the season. I take the new pickup, since it is still here and I have insured it.

My first two clients this year are a couple of older brothers from the Midwest somewhere and we hit it off well right from the start. They laugh and then sign my waivers and the hunt contracts and we are off. Our five days together are really fun and they both get lovely trophies to remember it by. Then they both contract me to make the rugs for them.

The weather even cooperates and we have fairly warm evenings with lovely sunny days. Most of the snow banks are gone by the time I take them back to town. We go to Fish & Game to get their hides and skulls tagged and then the airport and they are headed home. I stop at the tannery and drop off the hides. Then the Food Bank to drop off the meat.

I would drop my rates a bit if all my clients were as nice as those two. I know, that is one of those fairy tale dreams, so dream on.

My next clients aren't due in until late the day after next, so I do some grocery shopping and go home. I need some time at home this year, between clients.

The chicken coop needs cleaned and so does the litter box. Kivalina is happy to have me home and stays on my feet most of the time I am in the house.

The chickens are noncommittal, then I find some green sprouts of grass and pick them for the chickens and I am popular with them again. I have quite a pile of eggs in the box their nests empty into.

Once I get everything fairly well straightened up and the animals all happy again. I relax on the couch and have a lap kitty for the night, if I am willing to hold still. She has never been left alone before, usually Anuktuvik is here with her, at least. This is the part of hunt camps I am not pleased with.

Jeff stops by and asks if I need him to help in hunt camp. I tell him he can come if he wants, but it isn't necessary. He says he has three weeks off, so I tell him to come on out then, there is room. Since he is wanting to try for his Guide license as soon as possible, he needs several clients and a Guide he has worked under to write letters of approval for him before he can even apply to take the test. It is not easy to become a Guide up here.

Near camp

Chapter 23

I make it to the airport in plenty of time to pick up my next clients. We get the paperwork taken care of before leaving the airport. Then we stop and they purchase their licenses and tags. I ask them if they have any dietary preferences while we are still in town and can pick up anything needed.

We stop at the truck stop and have our evening meal. They both pick at their food and complain, so I have a feeling this is going to be a fun week. Then we drive on out to hunt camp and get them settled in. Jeff is already in camp and has coffee on. They complain about the coffee. He and I look at each other and decide this may be a quick hunt.

We each take one out and one gets a nice sized male bear this first night. Yes! Maybe we can get them done and back to town.

I set my sign on the table before starting breakfast. The first person to complain is the next cook. Usually that takes care of complaints. Neither one likes spices of any type, so I make as bland a breakfast as I can manage. Cream of rice and toast. Bleh.

This is the first meal neither one has complained about. Jeff and I may stage our own rebellion on the food if we have to eat like this all week. I set out stuff for everyone to make their own sandwiches for lunch.

They both pick white bread and plain smooth peanut butter, no jelly. Jeff and I both make a large sandwich complete with lunchmeat, onions, pickles, lettuce and tomatoes. They each take a bag of plain potato chips, we each grab the spicy chips. We talk a bit about what to have for dinner. They really like plain, so I put a roast and potatoes in a dutch oven, no spices, and sink it in the fire pit by the campfire to dig out this evening before we go hunting.

I put bottles of sauces on the table for Jeff and I to use on dinner and make some plain brown gravy from the pan juices when I dig it out. Dinner is filling and tender, but nothing special. The clients however, loved it. I guess as long as I keep it very plain and simple, they will be happy.

We only see small bears at the station so other than the client getting some nice photos, not much of an evening. When we get back to camp, they had some excitement. A young bear came through camp with a larger bear chasing it. If we had been here, the client might have filled his tag right in camp.

Breakfast is a redo of yesterday, so is lunch. I slice the leftover roast and heat it in the leftover gravy for hot roast beef sandwiches and mashed potatoes for dinner and am running out of bland ideas.

We go to the other bait station that night and just as we are about to call it a night, a very large old male comes wandering in and about gives my client a heart attack.

This is a ground stand and usually the bears come over and check us out before going to the bait. I had told my client that, but the reality of having a large bear looking at you from a few feet away is much different than listening to someone tell you about it. The client did manage to hold still and not stare into the bears eyes, so that was good, anyway.

The bear turned his back and lifted his leg on the end of the log we are sitting behind. Then walks over to the bait. When he turns sideways, I give the okay and the client makes a very good shot and drops the bear in his tracks.

We sit and have a bottle of water and a snack from my pack, then walk over to take care of his trophy. Before we start, we drag it quite a distance from the bait and the stand. I show him the best way to make his cuts if he wants the nicest looking rug from a bear. He gets in and helps skin so it doesn't take very long to complete our task. We partially skin out the head and feet before removing them from the body. We can finish them in the comfort of camp.

While he loads the hide on the 4 wheeler we came to the stand on, I clean up the station and make sure we left nothing behind. The meat is all loaded to haul in to the Food Bank after the clients were horrified to think of maybe eating some of it. We can have a lazy day in camp and then go to town a day early, if they like or we can go in tomorrow. They decide on going in tomorrow, so I better hurry on getting the feet and head skinned out.

Breakfast is again the bland stuff and I have some toast and start skinning the head and feet while Jeff starts packing gear to the truck. One of the clients is an amateur taxidermist and is going to do the hides himself, so they have to be fleshed a bit better and heavily salted.

I ask them if they want the hides tanned in Fairbanks and sent as soon as they are done, but they say no, they will do it at home. Okay, it is quite a job tanning bear hides. I have done it myself, and I prefer letting the tannery tan them before I do the rest of the work on them.

I drain the liquid off the salted hides and pack them in more salt and the best grade of plastic bag I have out here. The F&G office will still need to tag them., so can't pack for shipping. Not sure how they are going to do the skulls, I usually clean and mail them, but you can't mail them with meat on them.

Jeff wants to stick around camp while I am gone, so that is fine. I won't have to worry about anyone messing around with my camp while I am gone.

We load up the clients and their gear and I head to town. We don't see any game along the road on the way in and they are disappointed in not seeing a moose. I explain the cow hunt and they are upset. They say they will write letters about it when they get home. They turned out to be okay clients, even if they are picky eaters. We get the hides sealed and tagged at F&G and then find a hotel for them. They want to check out the museum and some other things while they are here. A lot of the things they want to do have not opened for the tourist season yet.

The skulls are now packed in a lined container and heavily salted. The hides are in larger containers and also heavily salted. Then everything is sealed up and ready to ship home. I take them over to UPS and they actually accept them. That will save a hassle at the airport. Art wanted to take his as carry on but it wouldn't fit in the size restrictions.

They now want to take me out to dinner, so we head to a nice out of town spot and actually enjoy a pleasant dinner. I drop them off at their hotel and head for home.

On my way home, I see three moose along the road. Wouldn't you know it?

Home, it looks so good just to be able to walk in, snuggle my cat and let the dog have free run without worrying that he is going to disturb a client. The chickens can wait until morning to be taken care of.

I have some emails waiting for me. Several from Jerry about my grandfather. My grandfather has recovered and is okay. He would like to come back for a visit. I answer them and remind him I am gone most of the week, every week, until bear season is over. An answer zings right back, so he must be on line right now. He wants to know if they can come spend time in hunt camp as they loved the hunt camp in the fall. I guess they can, they just have to realize the clients will always come first, in camp. So I write and tell him that. The answer is a bit slower coming back, but they accept the terms.

The pets and I tumble into bed and sleep totally uninterrupted the entire night. No worrying a bear is coming through the side of the tent or a client going off half cocked and shooting holes in the sky or closer. No matter how often I stress that no drugs or alcohol allowed in camp, some always manage to smuggle some in. Usually booze.

We are all up and dressed before Grant shows up. I have cleaned the litter box and shoveled the coop. Fresh water has been put in all drinking containers. So I am working on the greenhouse when he walks over.

I have buried plastic jugs upside down with a pinhole in the lid and the bottom cut out, to fill with water to water the greenhouse when I am gone. I add fertilizer through it once in a while. So the greenhouse is doing okay. The garden doesn't look so great. Most is planted and covered with clear plastic. It has a green haze of sprouted weed seeds under it.

I pull the plastic off carefully and till between the rows to at least keep some order in the garden. Then I start pulling little weeds in the rows. These I give the chickens and they love them. I know those won't be sprouting again if I just drop after pulling.

While Grant and I are standing here talking, a vehicle pulls in the driveway. It is Jerry and my grandfather. They must have an airline on speed dial.

Jerry gets me to one side and tells me he really wanted to get my grandfather away from the Lower 48. Rumors and innuendoes have led to some nasty incidents and he thinks Grampa will be safer here.

After last summer, I am not so sure and not so sure I want a repeat this year. But he is my grandfather, so yeah, he can stay.

They will stay in the same cabin they stayed in last winter. Grant and I finally got the rest of the roofing screws in the roofing and ridge caps on the two little cabins. My next trip in to town, I should pick up some plywood to finish the inside of both of them. Jerry says they will when they head back in for some supplies.

I still have a couple of days before the next clients come in, so I enjoy them completely. Anuktuvik can run around in the yard without having to be tied or shut in my truck and he is enjoying it very much. Kivalina is liking the lap time and snuggling at night. The chickens are enjoying fresh weeds. I'm just enjoying not having to keep anyone else happy as paying guests.

We all manage to give each other room and still get together for most evening meals and a bit of conversation before splitting up and going our own ways each evening. The day before picking up clients, I do a lot of baking. I make a lot of bread for camp and to leave here for Grant. I make some loaves of applesauce bread with nuts and some with raisins. They keep well, stay moist and usually are good to have in camp for snacks. I make a couple to leave here. Then I bake lots of cookies, peanut butter, oatmeal and chocolate chip seem to be everyone's favorites. I make enough to leave here, also.

I pack everything for camp in the pickup and go to town to pick up the next clients. They seem nice and we get the paperwork taken care of quickly. The licenses and tags take a bit longer as there is a line in the store at the counter we have to go to. They are getting fidgety. I truly hope they aren't normally fidgety, as they will probably never get a bear if they are.

They start fidgeting before we even get to the truck stop I usually buy dinner at, on our way out of town and it is only 15 miles into the trip. Oh man, this could be a long 5 days.

The service is a little slow this evening, but not bad and yes, there they go again. I am trying to figure out how I am ever going to get them to hold still on a stand without tranquilizers. If they won't take them, I sure will.

They must think "Are we there yet?" is a cute saying and by the time we are, they are lucky they are still riding on the inside of the pickup.

As I stomp over to camp, Jeff asks how the trip was. I tell him it was just fine until I picked up these two. Then Grampa and Jerry show up and the show gets on the road. Grampa tries to be patient but he is not a patient man. Jerry gets one of the clients off to the side and has a low conversation with him. His eyes bug out and he drags his mouthy buddy off to their tent. After a few hurried mumbles, there is quiet. The sound of quiet is so welcome, I don't even ask Jerry what he said to the client. No matter what he said, at the moment, I am thankful. Once I think it over a bit, I might not be so happy, but for tonight, it works for me.

After a couple of hours to settle down, I tap on the tree beside their tent and ask if they are ready to go out hunting tonight. They mutter a bit and ask why they have to hunt now, why not during the day. I explain the bears are out now and if they want to actually get one, they need to hunt at night. They ask how the bears can tell, since it isn't getting dark. Good question, but they can.

They finally emerge from the tent and Jeff and I each take one and head to our stands. I get the tree stand tonight and Jeff has the ground stand. We do see some bears but they are not coming in to the bait. The client is tapping his fingers on the railing.

I ask him if he has ever hunted before, he says yes, he has, but never had any luck. I tell him luck has nothing to do with it, just hold still or he won't be getting anything this trip, either. He is a bit huffy about it, but he is holding still when very large black bear comes in on the bait.

I tell him to wait for a broadside shot and inhale, exhale and hold his breath to slowly squeeze the trigger. He actually follows directions and has a very nice bear. His whoop of delight probably scared anything within a mile away from us. I pull a bag of homemade cookies out of my pack and some bottles of water and we sit and toast a job just beginning but a better understanding of hunting learned.

After waiting a few minutes, we climb down out of the tree stand and approach the bear from the back and poke it with the rifle barrel, ready to fire if needed. Then poke the eye and make sure. The client is so happy to finally harvest game that he has to tell me the whole story of his hunting life. He has hunted all over the world and never actually gotten anything before. No one ever told him to just hold still.

We drag the bear away from the station and skin it out. It is the last week we have to salvage the meat, so we place the quarters in game bags and load them on the 4 wheeler. The hide with head and feet still in place is rolled and placed on top and strapped down. Then we head back to camp.

Jeff and his hunter wander in a bit after we reach camp and we are still hanging the meat to cool and air. His partner can not believe he actually got a bear. He did not even see any small bears at the ground stand. I ask Jeff quietly after they have gone to their tent, how it went.

He said the man never held still. Toes tapped, fingers clicked, chair rocked back and forth. He expected him to start whistling any minute. I told him what I said to mine. He said if he had to take the man out the next night, he would try that. I tell him he doesn't have to, but he said now it is a challenge, he has to. If I can get a twitchy client a bear, he has to. It's for the honor of males everywhere. I cuff his shoulder and he laughs as he walks away.

I hear Jeff and his client long before they make it back to camp. The client does not sound happy and Jeff is adamant. When they get to camp I see what the problem is, right away. The client has shot one of the smallest but still legal bears I have ever seen. My dog is almost bigger than this bear.

Jeff says he told him not to shoot and the client shot anyway but after he got up to it and saw how small it really is, he wanted to dump it and go for a bigger bear.

Nope, not the way it works. If he wants to go buy another tag, he can continue to hunt, but he shot it, he bought it.

I skin it out and take care of the hide and skull. We name it Muffy in honor of another small bear shot years ago. The client is not happy, but they both have gotten their bears. As far as I am concerned, without purchasing another tag, they are done hunting. They do not wish to purchase another tag.

As soon as we are done with breakfast, we load up the clients and their gear and head for town. First stop, Fish & Game for getting sealed. The Inspector says the guy got lucky and his bear is legal, but just barely. I tell him it was shot over the objections of the Guide and he says he figured as much, since he only sees the little ones show up from either unguided hunts or people that ignore the Guide they paid so much to hunt with. Go figure.

They want the tanned hides sent to them at home, so I take them to the tannery. They take the hides in and he accepts their deposits and when he sees the little one, he smiles at me. He knows how that one was shot. He has worked some as a Guide, also.

They have a hotel lined up, so I drop them off there and stop at the grocery store for some fresh fruit. Then it is home for me.

Jerry and Grampa are back at their cabin when I pull in. Jeff says he is enjoying being out by himself, so stays on in camp. He only has another full week after this one off.

I enjoy having the rest of the week off. I love hunting and camping, but some clients really make me think about getting into another line of work. These two were not as bad as some and not as good as many more of my clients have been. All in all, it usually is a very nice business. I guess I always feel like doing something else after clients I don't much like.

As usual, the garden and greenhouse need work and I get on that. I think the chickens are actually listening for my footsteps as they flock the fence when I start throwing weeds over for them. One hen must have managed to hide her nest out of the boxes and in a corner where I don't normally look, because I have some new fluffy chicks in with the flock. The mother hen is a very large old hen, very territorial and protective, so the chicks stay apart from the others. I wasn't planning on more chickens, but it is like a lot of my plans. Subject to change without notice.

I start working on finishing the inside of the little cabins. Grampa and Jerry did bring out the plywood needed for wall paneling and it is nice working with all new materials. I finish up around the doors and windows with 1x4's and it looks pretty good. They could be rented out as overnight shelters and now I just need to put beds in them. I have some bed frames stored in the shed, so bring them over. One double bed at the end in each and a single bed along each side. I put a small table in each, near the door. They are not built for a comfortable stay, just a dry place to sleep instead of out in the weather, bugs and animals.

Jerry wanders over to see what the noise is about and looks it all over in surprise. Did he think I hired stuff done? I'm not exactly a hothouse flower.

We walk back over to my house together and he comes on in, with me. He asks me to take a seat so I do. Then he tells me my grandfather is very ill and it probably is terminal. He isn't telling me this to scare me, but to help me understand that my grandfather is enjoying being here and wants to spend as much time as possible getting to know me and maybe making up for never having been in my life. He asks that I allow my grandfather to indulge me if he wants to. He has never actually spent time with family before. He was an orphan. While he was married and before his wife died, he thought he had a lot of time later to spend with family but that didn't happen, then he alternately ignored and commanded his daughter until she ran away. He is trying to get it right.

I tell him I will try, but I am not going to be something I am not nor am I going to be manipulated into doing things I don't want to do.

He says he thinks my grandfather understands that now, since the deal with the pickup and he is glad to see I am now using it. We have been walking on egg shells a bit since that.

I thank him for the information and he leaves. I am just standing here, wondering what to fix for dinner when Grant comes by and asks if I would go out to dinner with him. Really? All the way to town for dinner? Really? Okay.

He says he will be back in a few minutes to pick me up. I rush through a quick shower and have my shoes on even, by the time he gets back. My hair is just put in a knot on the back of my head and I am wearing one of my few dresses and flat sandals. I don't think I could handle high heels. I grab a sweater off the peg by the door on my way out.

"Wow, is all I can say." Grant says as I come down the steps. He opens the pickup door for me and assists me into his pickup. Well, that is what he had in mind. I am so not used to being helped into vehicles. Sorry about the nose smack thing, wasn't expecting him that close when I hopped in.

Well, I sure hope the rest of the evening goes better than the start. Poor Grant is trying to delicately wipe his nose without being obvious about it. I hand him a tissue and tell him I am sorry, go ahead and blow.

We have dinner at a local place known for it's prime rib so of course I order the prawns. They are huge and delicious. Grant has the prime rib and says he has never had better. He had heard the other folks mention the food here and just didn't want to come by himself. Gee, that makes me feel special. He stops and thinks how that sounded and tries to correct it, making it worse, so I grin at him and tell him I understand, and just enjoy the food and be quiet.

We are both so stuffed by the time we leave, that we almost roll to the pickup. Then he drives over to another place well known for their desserts. Oh wow, we should have stopped here first. No, dinner was excellent but I am going into overload now.

When we go in, they have dancing on one side and the restaurant on the other, so we spend some time dancing, first, until we both decide maybe we can handle some dessert now. The offerings are rich and decadent looking, so we each order something different and will share both for variety.

I get a slice of dark chocolate raspberry cheesecake and Grant orders a slice of blueberry swirl cheesecake using our wild berries. I cut off a piece of mine and slide it to his plate and he does the same. I try his first and it is delicious but oh my, when I try mine. That has to be the best cheesecake I have ever eaten. Grant seems happy with his though, so maybe he isn't as much into chocolate as I am.

We savor each bite and it takes a while to finish our desserts. We dance a while before going back out to the pickup and heading home.

Grant says he can not get used to the daylight, 24/7. He said winter didn't bother at all, but the steady daylight does. He has put room darkening shades over all the windows in his cabin so he can sleep.

When he drops me off at my house, Grant thanks me for a fun evening and says we should do it again, soon. Maybe all but the nose bump part.

I do some baking for the next crop of clients due in tomorrow, and then prepare dinner for everyone here. Grant has fixed up the woodshed by his place and it is a nice little enclosed picnic area for the summer. He is stockpiling firewood beside it to be moved inside in the fall. He is on permanent leave of absence unless he ever wants to go back and is seriously trying to make a living on his writing now. From what I have read for him, he does a darn good job of it, too. We eat dinner in the woodshed.

He says he is not up to the level of income he had with the police, but he enjoys it far more and doesn't have the expenses he had there, either. He asks about renting for a longer period of time, say a year at a time? Why not, we get along okay, he helps out often and it is rather nice having someone on the place if I have to go somewhere. I tell him sure. We can print out a contract later.

Now that Jerry has told me that Grampa is ill, I notice small things I never paid attention to before. Some weight loss and some weakness once in a while as he starts to do something, pauses and then goes ahead. I continue to bake fattening things and he does eat them. So his appetite is still pretty good. The rest of us will have to watch it though, we will be gaining while he just holds steady.

He asks if I ever plan on having a family and I tell him sure, one of these days. He tells me he likes and approves of all the young men that he has met around here. Does he realize he has met only policemen here? I don't think so. But they are a nice lot and I like them all, too. It's just that I don't like them in quite the way he wants me to like one. For that matter, until he mentioned it, I hadn't thought of any of them in that way. We were just people working together. Except a few drools over Grant.

.Dang, now that he has planted the notion in my head, I am looking at each one as a potential life partner. I doubt highly if any of them have looked at me in that way, either. Oh well, other things to do, it will be something to think about later, much later.

Chapter 24

When I go in to pick up the next clients, Grampa asks if he can ride along. Sure, there is room. He, Anuktuvik and I have the front seat and the clients get the back seat, works for me.

One of the clients evidently fancies himself a special gift to women. Maybe if they are into loud mouthed, beer bellied, balding fellows, he might be. This might be a long week. I hope Grampa doesn't decide the fellow needs lessons in manners. I whisper this to him and he says he will let me handle it unless I ask him to take care of it.

By the time we reach hunt camp, I am gritting my teeth to keep from saying something I may regret later. The guy does the gentlemanly thing and helps balance the load I am packing to the camp from the truck by placing his carry on bag on top the load I already have. What a guy.

Jeff and Grampa are both damaging their teeth holding their mouths shut so tightly before we settle in around the fire for dinner. After dinner, I assign the Lothario to Jeff for the evening hunt. The client is not happy, I guess he had visions of he and I alone on our stand doing whatever his warped mind was thinking.

He grabbed my arm as I walked by to swing me around and found himself flat on the ground with my foot in his armpit and his hand twisted around to the point one ounce of pressure and he would have been looking at a dislocated or broken arm. The look on his face is priceless. I hiss at him that the first rule of the camp is Do. Not. Touch. Me. Ever.

Grampa's jaw has dropped and Jeff is smiling hugely. The other client is smiling a bit, too. I ease up on the man's hand and he starts to yank away, but I haven't let go yet and he is back where he started and in a bit of pain. Now I need only a half ounce of pressure to really hurt him. I ask if he understands what I am telling him. His face has gone white and he nods his head yes.

I slowly release the pressure on his hand and arm and step back. He is much slower to try getting up this time. I walk on over to the client I will take hunting and we head out for our stand.

We have a good evening for viewing younger bears and he takes a lot of video and photos. Nothing very large comes in on the station and we finally call it a night and head for camp. He warns me about his partner. He will be looking for a chance to get even with me for not only resisting him but for humiliating him in front of others. I thank him for the warning and take Anuktuvik in the tent with me when I go to bed.

Some time during the night, something outside the

tent makes Anuktuvik growl a deep rumbly growl in his throat and I hear a mumbled curse outside and then footsteps leaving the area around my tent. Some people never learn.

The clients seem a bit grumpy when they come out of the tent for breakfast. The one I am taking out is not pleased with his partner. I keep out of the man's way most of the day and when it is time to head out for the stands, he is trying to change guides with his partner.

Somehow, two of the 4 wheelers won't start, so it looks like we have to double up to ride to the stands and he is thinking that is one way to get his hands on me. Not happening.

I still send him and Jeff out on the two remaining ATVs. I check and the spark plugs are loose on the other two, so I fix them and soon we are on our way, also.

Jeff and his client actually get a bear and a nice sized one at that. My client and I see a nice very large bear, but it never comes out of the brush enough to get a clear shot. Neither one of us wants to track a wounded bear, so we are both very willing to wait until there is a clear shot.

The next night, the same bear stays around the bait, but never comes on in. We do this for three nights and by now, the bear must think we are harmless, because he comes right in about an hour after we get on site. That's what we were waiting for and my client has a very nice trophy to remember this hunt by. He says next time he will come up with a different hunt partner. His usual hunting partner was ill and sent this one in his place. They had not even met before.

I tell him I would enjoy having him come back as a client for a hunt any time. I, too, would rather never hunt with his partner again. I am just glad Jeff was still here for this hunt.

When we get back to camp, the other client is very quiet and subdued. I guess Grampa took him aside when he was talking about what he would like to be doing with me, and gave him some advice. Suddenly he is a very quiet man and does not even look at me. I wonder just what Grampa said to him? It must have been good.

After taking care of the hides better and scraping down the skulls more, putting a lot of salt on them and packing in moisture proof containers, we head to town. Evidently, the clients have had a falling out also, so they want dropped at different hotels after we get the hides and skulls sealed at F&G.

We drop the obnoxious one first. Then the other one says he would like me to take care of making his rug, so we go over to the tannery to drop off his hide and he makes the arrangements and prepays for it. He gives me a good deposit on the rug, also, so that is very nice. He asks if he can take me out to dinner as a thank you and apology for his poor judgment in letting the obnoxious one come along. He was going to have some words with his usual partner about his choice as substitute.

While we are having dinner, his cell phone rings

and I tell him to go ahead and answer it. It is his usual hunting partner and he jumps right in asking why he sent that jerk. The man also apologizes and it turns out the jerk is that guys' brother-in-law. When he couldn't go, his wife volunteered her brother. He was hoping we would forgive him and offered to send me something to make up for the putting up with the jerk. My client tells him what I did. I can hear laughter clear across the table. He asks his friend if he caught it on camera. He would pay big bucks for the clip and post it on the internet. He is sorry the chance was missed and asks if I would be willing to do it again for the camera. Um, no.

I wonder if the man acts that way at home. In today's PC world, he is aching for harassment lawsuits. I should have taken him out hunting, but I was afraid I would permanently hurt him.

After dinner, I drop the man at his hotel and wish him a safe trip home. As he is getting out of my pickup, the other client is waiting for him inside and comes out with attitude. I am just setting the bags on the sidewalk when the idiot grabs my arm yet again.

This time, since he had his phone out already, there are going to be pictures and maybe video of the event.

Yet again, loudmouth is looking up at me from flat on his back with his arm, twisted around and my foot on his armpit.

He starts yelling profanities and I apply a wee bit

of pressure. He stops.

What is with this guy? Does he think this is some sort of fun?

I continue our conversation with my client and he thanks me for a good hunt. I slowly ease back on the idiot on the ground and let go, then hop into my pickup and drive off.

The next morning, Jim and Teri stop and inform me that the idiot wanted to press charges against me. Then his partner pulled up the video. He already has it posted on internet. With sound. He started recording when he saw the man coming through the doors and has the whole works recorded. Jeff pulls in while they are still here. He asks what the problem is and they tell him. He has some choice words for that client. He tells them how the whole time in camp went and he can't believe the guy tried it again. Jim has it on his laptop and shows the whole thing to Jeff.

I don't think we are going to get any guide recommendations from that client. Just my finely honed guiding instinct tells me that.

Jerry and Grampa pull in and Jeff takes Jim's laptop over to share with them. Grampa seems a bit put out that the man went ahead and even touched me again after the little pep talk he had with him in camp. I hope we convinced Grampa that it was going to be punishment enough having it on the internet. Grampa still has friends near this guys' home town. Grampa can be a bit vindictive.

Grampa asks me where I learned to put someone

down like that. I tell him about the place in Fairbanks, the Arctic Athletics Association. Those guys really know how to teach self defense. He wants to go meet them.

Jeff has to go back to town in a couple of days. I'm certainly going to miss his help with the clients in camp the rest of bear season. He wants to come back for moose season. I sure won't complain, he will make an excellent Guide when he gets his own license. He says he has put in for moose season off.

I do the usual stuff around the place until it is time to pick up my next clients. These are hunters I have guided before and we will have an excellent week. I am looking forward to seeing them.

Since I made notes in past years on likes and dislikes, I know these two love anything chocolate, so I meet them with a bag of brownies in the back seat for them to munch on, on our way out. We get the paperwork signed, the licenses and tags and are on our way.

Grampa has decided he likes riding back and forth with me, so he is along on our trip, also. Jerry is at the camp. We stop at the truck stop for dinner and get a take out to give Jerry when we get there, that is if we can keep Anuktuvik's nose out of the bag.

We have an easy and unremarkable hunt. We all have so much fun it is a shame to see them go. We wait until we have to leave to get the hides and skulls sealed at F&G, then drop the hides at the tannery. We even make it to the airport just in time for them to catch their flight. Some clients become friends and I hate to see them go.

I have to scramble to get ready for the next weeks' clients. They will be the last for this season. Then it is time to clean up the camp site and the stands come down and clean up around them.

Grampa and I make it to the airport in time to pick up the clients and they are also repeat customers. They don't really want to get anything, they just want to take pictures, so we sign the paperwork, but no licenses or tags. One decides to go ahead and get a license, but no tag. I ask him why the license and he says he just wants to have one. He has had an Alaskan license for the last 10 years and doesn't want to stop now. Well, okay.

We go out together to the tree stand and they set up the cameras they have brought. The first three nights, they get some really good video, the fourth night, we get something none of us were expecting. A huge sow comes in by herself and soon there are two large males pushing and shoving at each other. Then they get into a all out brawl and the clients get it all on video.

We wait a while after they have all gone. The loser will be in a very bad humor and we don't want to run across him now. The winner will be territorial, so we don't want to find him, either.

We have one more evening of possible filming. They decide to go for it and we head back to the tree stand. Somehow I feel safer up in the trees with me being the only one with a gun, with the pair of large black bears and the disgruntled loser.

However, they become the least of our problems. A huge grizzly comes slowly meandering through the trees to the station. Oh yikes, I really don't want this.

The fellows have the cameras going but we are all being very quiet and not moving. It's a good thing we charged up their batteries with the pickup today. They are going to have some extra special home movies to show out of this. The grizzly finally wanders off and we climb down and head for camp. It isn't all that late in the evening, but we are not going to top that one.

We leave for town after stopping at my place for a while. They graciously offer me a copy of all they have taken and we download it onto my laptop. Then we burn three DVDs of it, so they have one each just in case they lose the footage somewhere between here and home. They can edit and tweak it all once they are home. They are so happy with the whole experience that they tip me as though they had each gotten a huge trophy and in a lot of ways, this is better than any other trophy could be.

When I drop these clients at the airport, we are all sad to see this trip end. We have enjoyed the camaraderie of camp and good meals, plus the thrill of seeing magnificent animals.

When I am settled at home this evening, I burn another DVD for Grampa to have at his cabin to watch any time he wants to. He loves seeing the animals.

Chapter 25

After a good late breakfast, Grant, Grampa, Jerry and I all go back to clean up the bait stations. With the bears we have seen hanging around them lately, there is safety in numbers. It doesn't take us long to drop the stink buckets hanging high above each station to waft scent on every breeze. We cap them tightly and roll the bait barrels to the 4 wheelers, load everything up and haul it back to camp. The chairs and camouflage nets are folded up and loaded in the pickup.

Disassembling the tree stand takes a bit longer, but it is finally loaded and hauled to camp, also. The tents are down and the fire ring is disassembled and scattered, the fire pit for cooking filled back in. By the time we leave, there isn't much left to show we have lived here for 2 months.

Once we get everything home, I hang the tents over clotheslines to air them out really well and dry the bottoms. The sleeping bags we used are hung out to air, also. I always bring extra to camp in case a client doesn't have one, but most bring their own. Then I remember the roll that dropped out of one of the bags after the fall hunt. I go inside and it is still under the coats on the coat rack.

Jerry is surprised and happy to see it. It is some important papers he was supposed to take home with them and forgot in our hurry to leave camp last fall.

I heat up some soup and have the sandwich supplies left from camp, so when the others stop by, there is food, but it isn't a great meal for all the work that was done today. I do pull out a cheesecake I picked up in town before coming home yesterday and we have that for dessert. Maybe that makes up for the skimpy meal.

Teri and Sheila show up right after breakfast. Teri has the day off and she and Sheila have become friends. They assure me no shots, fires or explosions have occurred during their friendship or while Sheila stayed with Teri when she first was released from the hospital.

They say that Cary is still not doing well but is in custody in Fairbanks. He was injured too much internally to ever fully recover. He knows he might not make it, so actually is working with the police now to figure it all out. Basically, he tells a simple story.

Cary flew as far as San Francisco. There was a fairly long layover between flights, so he catches a budget flight back with fake ID, kills William Garrison The Third, another budget flight back to San Francisco, then catches his flight north to Fairbanks. He rented a room for the rest of that night and made sure people saw him. Then he goes looking for me to finish up his alibi. I even make it easy by spotting his ticket and pointing it out to the police in the tire shop.

McCready was part of a mob connection, infiltrating William Garrison The Thirds' casino investments and laundering money through William Garrison The Third's company. The Third was catching on and the Mob had outstanding debt against Cary. He was blackmailed into getting rid of The Third with threats against his step sister, Sheila. McCready got greedy and wanted more of the proceeds from the casinos or to step into William Garrison The Thirds shoes, to handle them and was trying to blackmail his mob boss and had his evidence on a flash drive. The flash drive is still missing and no one knows where it is.

At this point, Sheila hesitantly stands up and says she knows where the flash drive is. Teri about has a heart attack. Grant is perked up like a bird dog on point. Grampa and Jerry have been listening to everything as though it were a drama on TV. No flicker of personal interest convinces me and I think, Grant, that there is no personal involvement with the events they are listening to.

She says she found the flash drive when Cary, McCready and her were still staying in the main cabin. She saw it fall out of McCready's jacket when he was picking it up and she scooted a piece of paper over it. After he and Cary stepped outside, she picked it up and pocketed it, then came over here to visit me.

She wanted to retrieve it the last time she came out, but the board is now screwed down. As soon as she said that, I know where the flash drive is.

I grab the screw gun and we all troop out to my outhouse. Only one board on the whole place is screwed down, so it isn't a mystery. I am busy with the screw gun and don't even hear the SUV pulling up in my yard. Evidently, everyone else is too busy watching to pay attention either. The first thing that finally gets my attention is the gunshot.

That totally gets my attention and I drop the screw gun and stand up. The person wearing a ski mask yells at me to continue what I am doing and everyone else but Sheila get back and hold still or we both get it. He isn't even original. The voice sounds familiar and I am trying to place it. He tosses Jerry a roll of duct tape and tells him to tape everyone's hands behind them. This does not look like a good situation, any way I look at it.

I do happen to be armed, but it is one of the belts that I, um, liberated a few months ago. I would have to be really close and only have 2 shots with it, and not easy to aim my belly and haven't had time to practice with it. While I am working the screw loose, I am also releasing the lock on the belt gun.

The board finally comes loose and Sheila reaches in to retrieve the flash drive. It is in a waterproof container and she opens the case, takes out the drive and removes the outer cover, puts the flash drive back in the waterproof container and drops it down the outhouse hole and grabs the little case it had been in. The girl is fast. If I had not seen her do that, I would have thought she was fumbling a bit getting it out from under the board.

She has seen me undo the gun and then hands me the case so I have an excuse to get close to him. When we walk out, the man has Jerry hand Sheila the tape to tape his hands. She does, but I see that she has the tape backwards so it isn't sticking to his skin and he can work it around if he is careful. This girl thinks fast on her feet. The man motions me over with the flash drive and I have the little gun in my other hand, fully covered. It is hard to believe it isn't a toy, it is so small.

His eyes leave me temporarily as he reaches for the flash drive and I shoot him. Sheila, Jerry and I immediately all tackle him and Grant is right in there even though he can't get his hands loose yet. Jerry taped them but not tightly, so he soon has them free also.

The man seems too familiar I have to rip the mask off and it is my obnoxious client of the bear hunts, George Johnson.

He is moaning and we have his gun now and Sheila is busy untaping Teri and Grampa.

I think I might have to rethink not letting her come around. Yeah, there were shots fired, but she is quick thinking and a big help. No fires or explosions though, this time. Of course, there is the flash drive down the outhouse hole to retrieve.

She says that shouldn't be too big a problem, if I have a good flashlight and a bucket. I go in for a headlamp and we look down the hole. There is the waterproof container, floating on top of the water that hasn't gone down from spring thaw. Eewww.

I go find an old bucket and some rope. We tie the rope on the handle and lower the bucket and then try to manage to catch the floating container in the bucket. It sounds easy. I finally get a long stick and we take turns trying to poke the container into the bucket until we finally make it. We take the icky bucket and contents out and dump it on the ground. Then we both haul water over and dump a lot of it on the container to rinse it well. This has been a crappy case all along.

I find some rubber gloves in the house that I use for skinning and open the container to get the flash drive out. Grant has the cover from George Johnson and is placing the flash drive back in the cover. Teri has the restraints out of her car and on George, so he can't pull some other stupid stunt. John McCready had been married to his other sister. I feel sorry for my client's friend this one came up in place of, if his sisters are anything like him.

Teri and Grant will take George in to the hospital then jail for him. The dinky little gun only gouged out a piece across his ribs, but it shocked him enough to give us a chance to take him down.

Sheila asks if she can stay a few days and I tell her sure. There were only a couple of gunshots this time.

Grampa is upset that he didn't get a chance to have a one on one talk with George. He figures

George needs to be taught some manners. He asks me about the little gun as he has seen them before and it was not a good memory. So I take him aside and tell him how I got them. Them? I have more than one? Uh, yes,. I got two that day, would he like one to wear? Yes, yes he would. You never know when you might need one.

www.ingramcontent.com/pod-product-compliance
Lightning Source LLC
Chambersburg PA
CBHW060639260626
47161CB00008B/2919